DOCTOR WHO AND THE
POWER OF KROLL

DOCTOR WHO
AND THE
POWER OF KROLL

Based on the BBC television serial by Robert Holmes
by arrangement with the British Broadcasting
Corporation

TERRANCE DICKS

A TARGET BOOK
published by
the Paperback Division of
W. H. ALLEN & Co. Ltd

A Target Book
Published in 1980
by the paperback division of W. H. Allen & Co. Ltd
A Howard & Wyndham Company
44 Hill Street, London W1X 8LB

Printed in Great Britain by
Richard Clay (The Chaucer Press), Ltd.,
Bungay, Suffolk

ISBN 0 426 20101 9

Contents

Prologue

Deep beneath the waters of the immense lagoon, Kroll slept.

He lay dormant, as he had lain for hundreds of years, buried in the thick nutritious sediment that covered the bottom of the lake.

His feeding tentacles radiated out from the great bulbous body, absorbing nourishment like the spreading roots of some enormous tree.

The years passed by, and still Kroll slept. His body-cells mutated, transformed by the strange power-source he carried deep within him. Kroll *grew* to colossal, unimaginable size. Yet still he slept.

Above him, the People of the Lakes paddled silently through the marshes in their canoes, and worshipped the image of Kroll in their temples—though none still living had seen him.

One day great changes came to Kroll's lagoon. Men came in rocket ships, and unloaded strange machines. They built a structure of towering steel on the very edge of Kroll's lagoon. Its waters were disturbed by the sound of their machinery, a thudding vibration that penetrated even the depths where Kroll had slept so long.

Kroll woke—and found that he was hungry.

Prompted by some long-dormant instinct, Kroll began his long slow rise.

There was life on the surface—and to Kroll, all life was food.

I

The Swamp

It was a world of water.

Lagoons the size of seas covered most of its surface, so that the swampy, low-lying land masses were in constant danger of flooding. Water streamed from perpetually overcast grey skies, in rain showers which ranged from the mildest drizzles to torrential downpours. Even when it wasn't raining, water seemed to hang in the air in an ever-present haze.

It was no place for men—but men lived there all the same.

The shuttle craft touched down on the Refinery's tiny landing pad, discharged its solitary passenger and his bulging travel-bag, and took off as if it couldn't wait to get away again.

Thawn stood looking for a moment at the Refinery. It was built on a steel-legged platform high above the waters of the lagoon. There were gleaming metallic domes and towers; a maze of intake pipes that coiled down from the processing plant and disappeared beneath the lagoon, prefabricated plasti-steel cabins forming the control area and living quarters.

Thawn stood for a moment, drawing in deep breaths

of the local air. It hadn't changed. Warm, moisture-laden, the perpetual hint of rotting vegetation. He smiled. It was good to be back.

He was a tall, heavily built man, with broad shoulders, long arms and enormous hands. His big-jawed, heavily moustached face gave him a rather menacing look. He stood for a moment longer, looking at the Refinery—his Refinery. Then he picked up his travel-bag, walked over to the little dock, where a number of canoe-like craft were moored. Thawn tossed his bag in the nearest and paddled out to the Refinery platform.

Inside the Refinery itself, there were bright lights, metal walls, air conditioning, the perpetual throb of machinery. Thawn made his way to central control, a semi-circular metal-walled chamber lined with instrument banks, dominated by the central console with its radar and viewing screens.

His crew were waiting for him. They hadn't changed either. Fenner, dark, round-faced with a look of irritable gloom, as though he had some perpetual grudge against life. Dugeen, young and eager, yet with an air of nervous tension. Harg, amiable enough, but often quiet and withdrawn.

Thawn himself tended to be silent and uncommunicative, so they weren't exactly a happy band of brothers. But they were all expert at their jobs and they worked well together, an efficient team. Like

Thawn, they wore the blue and white uniforms of the Government Scientific Service.

As usual, Dugeen sat hunched over his radar screen.

Fenner was checking instrument readings, and he looked up as Thawn came in. 'Hello, Controller. Saw you land. How did things go on Delta Magna?'

'Very well.' Thawn smiled briefly, as if at some private thought. 'Very well indeed. It was a useful trip. Place is getting very crowded, though. You notice that, after a few months here.'

Delta Magna was their home world, a bustling, heavily industrialised planet. Reasonably Earth-like, it had been one of the first to be colonised. Now, like Earth itself, it was over-developed to the point where its teeming population was running out of both space and food. Hence this Refinery.

Thawn fished inside his travel-bag and handed a small parcel to Harg. 'Here you are, your micro-cassettes. I got you the whole library, all five hundred books.'

'That's marvellous, sir. How much do I owe you?'

'Don't worry, we'll work it out later.'

Fenner touched a button, and a humanoid shuffled into the room. He wore a simple uniform of coarse, grey material, and his skin was green. His name was Mensch, and he was a Swampie, one of the planetoid's native inhabitants. None of the four men in the room spared him a glance.

Mensch was carrying a tray of plastic cups. Fenner nodded towards it. 'Care for a drink?'

'Thanks.' Thawn took one of the cups, drained the fiery local brandy in a gulp, shuddered and tossed the cup back on the tray. 'Out!' he barked. The Swampie scuttled away, and stood watching in the doorway.

'Hey!' said Dugeen suddenly. 'What's going on here?'

Fenner looked round. 'What's the matter, did you want a drink too?'

Dugeen shook his head impatiently. 'There's something odd on my radar, a sort of echo track.'

'Check it again,' said Fenner indifferently.

'I've checked. I've checked it five times. Look!'

The others drifted over to the radar screen.

'Here, look at this. I'll play it back for you.'

Dugeen touched a control and a spot of light moved slowly across the screen. 'That's you coming in, Controller, about twelve miles out. Now, look, this is where the other track starts to show.'

Suddenly a smaller spot of light separated from the first, streaked off on a different course, and disappeared off the edge of the screen.

'What do you think it is?'

'I think you were followed here, sir. Someone used your radar track as cover, and split off at the very last minute.'

'It's another ship all right,' said Fenner slowly. 'It must have landed in the swamp somewhere.'

Dugeen looked up at Thawn. 'The scanners were set to monitor your ship's approach to the pad, sir. Any secondary plot was irrelevant.'

'But who'd risk it?' asked Harg. 'Nothing out there but swamp and wasteland anyway.'

Thawn said abruptly, 'Now listen to me all of you. This could be serious. When I was on Delta Magna, I got a warning from Government Intelligence. The Sons of Earth are planning to arm the Swampies.'

Fenner groaned. 'There are times I could well do without the Sons of Earth.'

'Couldn't we all,' said Harg wearily.

The Sons of Earth were a well-organised pressure group back on Delta Magna. They took the view that man, having hopelessly polluted his native Earth, was going on to repeat the same process on a variety of other worlds. Delta Magna itself was already in danger. Now the scientists and technicians were spreading their attentions to its moons, and in particular to this one.

The Sons of Earth were of the opinion that this process should be stopped; they were getting increasingly militant about the ways in which it should be done.

Delta Three was a sore point with them, because of the Swampies.

Originally, the Swampies had been the native inhabitants of Delta Magna itself. When swarms of colonising Earthmen had over-run their planet, the Swampies had been shipped off to one of its satellites. Delta Three was a desolate watery planetoid, then thought to be useless. The Swampies had been deported there, much as the Red Indians of Earth had been sent off to reservations in America. They had been promised that the little world should be theirs, and theirs alone. But the scientists on Delta Magna had found a use for Delta Three after all, and the Refinery had been set up. If it was successful, there would be more refineries and still more, until Delta Three was as industrialised as Delta Magna itself, and the Swampies would be homeless once again.

It was not a point which greatly concerned most of those in the control centre. Thawn in particular had been the driving force behind the Refinery scheme in the first place. He had done the preliminary survey, and persuaded the Government to set up the scheme. Now his career as a scientist depended on its success.

In Thawn's view, the Swampies were no more than obstacles in the way of progress. Even the mild-mannered Harg seemed to agree with him. 'Arm the Swampies? Oh, but surely nobody would give guns to those savages?'

No one so much as glanced at the Swampie servant in the doorway.

Thawn said sternly, 'Don't you believe it. Those savages are getting a lot of sentimental support back on Delta Magna. Oh, the Government public relations people are putting a lot of effort into giving a more balanced picture . . . But you've got to remember, most people on Delta Magna have never even seen a Swampie. You can imagine the sort of thing that's being said. "Noble savages" deprived of their homelands for the second time.'

'Even so, sir, it's unthinkable,' protested Harg. 'If

the Swampies were given guns, it could lead to them attacking the Refinery.'

'That's exactly what it would lead to,' said Thawn grimly.

Dugeen said, 'But the Sons of Earth have always condemned violence, Controller. Surely they wouldn't be likely to arm the Swampies?'

'I'm not so sure. There was also an Intelligence report that Rohm Dutt's ship had vanished from Port Elevedor. All stations have been told to keep a look out for him.'

'Rohm Dutt? He's a gun-runner, isn't he?'

'That's right,' said Fenner.

'Do you really think that it was *his* ship that followed Controller Thawn?'

'I don't know,' said Fenner slowly. 'But if it *is* him, he'll be heading for the main Swampie Settlement. He'll have to go into the swamps.'

Thawn didn't seem very worried. 'Well, in that case he may never reach the Settlement at all.'

Fenner said agitatedly, 'I think we ought to go and look for him, sir, try to cut him off. If he is bringing guns for the Swampies, we're all in very great danger.'

'All right, Fenner, if you like. But you know how big those swamps are—and how dangerous. Even if it is Rohm Dutt—he probably won't reach the Settlement alive.'

'Still, we'd better take a look, Controller. Even if the Swampies kill him and *take* the guns, the results will be the same as far as we're concerned.'

Thawn yawned, and stretched. 'All right, all right. We'll take the hovercraft.'

Fenner hurried away, and Thawn followed him.

Thawn had been curiously unperturbed by the whole incident, thought Dugeen. Usually any threat to his beloved Refinery had him in an instant rage ...

No, thought Dugeen, there was something very odd about Thawn's reaction ...

There was a wheezing groaning sound in the swamp, and a square blue police box appeared on top of a little hillock of firm ground. The door opened and a tall curly-haired man came striding out. He wore a comfortably loose jacket, an immensely long trailing scarf, and a battered old soft hat with a very wide brim. Behind him was a dark-haired, elegantly beautiful girl, in trousers and a bright orange tunic. Both wore high waterproof boots against the ever-present mud. The tall man was that mysterious traveller in Time and Space known as the Doctor, the girl his companion, a Time Lady called Romana.

They had come to Delta Three on a mission that affected the safety of the entire universe.

They were looking for one of the missing segments of the Key to Time.

The Doctor and Romana had been given a vital mission by the White Guardian, one of the most powerful and mysterious beings in the cosmos.

Long ago, the Key to Time had been split into six

parts. They were scattered to different parts of the universe, in order to prevent so powerful an object falling into the hands of any one being.

Now the balance of the cosmos was being threatened by the evil Black Guardian, and only the Key to Time could restore it. The Doctor and Romana had been despatched to find the six missing segments and assemble them once more.

The task was complicated by the fact that the segments had many strange powers, including that of transmutation. They could look like virtually anything, from a jewelled pendant to an enormous statue.

To assist them in their task, the Doctor and Romana had been given the Tracer, a slender wand-like device with a number of extraordinary powers. Plugged into the TARDIS console, it could lead them, one by one, to the widely scattered planets in which the segments could be found.

Once they arrived, the Tracer could be detached and used like a kind of mine-detector, leading them to the exact spot where the segment could be located. Finally, when touched by the Tracer, the segment reverted to its true form—a large irregularly shaped chunk of crystal.

Romana was looking around her with an expression of pronounced distaste. They were in the middle of a swamp. There was nothing to be seen but miles and miles of reed-beds stretching in every direction, broken up by hundreds of meandering streams, some wide, some narrow, and the occasional muddy track.

Here and there were little clumps of higher ground, like the one they were standing on now. The sky was grey, everything was damp and soggy. It had obviously just been raining, and it looked as if it was going to rain again at any moment. There was no sound except the mournful sighing of the wind in the reed-beds, and the occasional gurgling and sucking of the swamp.

Just ahead of them a channel, wide enough to be called a river, cut through the marshes.

'Really, Doctor! Was it absolutely necessary to land in the middle of a quagmire?'

The Doctor was studying the marshy landscape with cheerful interest. 'Told you it was going to be swampy. Anyway, it's not my fault. Or the TARDIS's, is it, old girl?' He gave the police box a consoling pat. 'Looks as if these marshes go on for miles and miles. Still, a little water never hurt anybody.'

'Try telling that to K9. He's marooned now, poor old chap.'

K9 was the Doctor's other companion. In appearance a kind of robot dog, K9 was in reality a mobile self-powered computer. He had all kinds of extraordinary powers, but the one thing he couldn't cope with was water. Damp had a disastrous effect on his circuits.

'Never mind,' said the Doctor cheerfully. 'With any luck we won't be here long enough to need K9.' He threw his hat in the air, and studied its fall.

Romana stared at him. 'What *are* you doing, Doctor?'

'Gravity check,' said the Doctor with dignity. 'Escape velocity about one point five miles per second.'

'Really? That's a bit low for a planet, isn't it?'

'Yes. We're on a planetoid, one of the moons of Delta Magna. Delta Three to be precise.' He picked up his hat and put it on again.

'Doctor, sometimes I wonder if you're quite right in the head,' said Romana exasperatedly.

'Well, don't worry about me. Just point the Tracer and see where we head for next.'

Romana produced the Tracer from inside her tunic and held it up. Instead of its usual clear electronic note, it produced a blurred, fuzzy sound. 'That's odd. It's not giving a clear reading. It seems to cover a spread of about forty-two and a half degrees.'

'I don't like the sound of that,' said the Doctor. 'Either we're right on top of the thing—which we're not—or the Tracer's developed a fault.'

Romana looked around. 'Maybe the damp in the atmosphere's affecting it. I'll just go over to the higher ground over there and try again.' She pointed to a nearby hillock, considerably larger than the one where they were standing. 'There seems to be a path—of sorts.'

'Yes, why don't you try that? I'll wait here.'

Romana disappeared into the reed-beds and the Doctor stood waiting, hands in pockets, whistling idly. So tall were the reeds that they rose over Romana's head. For a while the Doctor could follow her track by the rustling of the reeds, then he lost sight of her.

He studied the reeds close to him thoughtfully, and fished an old clasp-knife from his pocket. Opening the blade, he selected a reed with care and cut it off at the base. Happily he began carving himself a flute . . .

Romana trudged along the muddy path which was so narrow that the rustling reeds seemed to crowd in on her. She had a moment of panic, wondering if she'd get lost, then reflected that the Doctor was near enough to hear her if she yelled. The path began to rise . . .

Romana heard a faint rustling sound. She paused, listening. A green hand clamped over her mouth, a green arm wound round her neck, and she was dragged swiftly and silently into the reed-beds.

2

The Gun-Runner

The Refinery hovercraft sped along one of the many rivers that criss-crossed the Swamplands. Hovercraft were the only practicable forms of transport on Delta Three, since the marshy, waterlogged ground made road building difficult. So, on the rare occasions when they had to leave the Refinery, Thawn and his fellow technicians used the hovercraft, speeding over water and swamp with a roar of jet-engines.

(Swampies used boats when they travelled the swamplands, slender, canoe-like affairs that glided silently through the innumerable tiny channels.)

Thawn and Fenner were covering the main waterways in a methodical search pattern, looking for the renegade gun-runner, Rohm Dutt. If he was bringing a cargo of guns to the Swampies, he would have to travel with a fairly large party, and there were only so many routes to the Settlement. He shouldn't be too hard to find.

Fenner raised his voice above the roar of the hovercraft. 'What does he look like, this Rohm Dutt?'

Thawn sat slumped in the driving seat, his big hands resting confidently on the guiding-wheel. 'Rohm

Dutt? He likes to think he's a bit of a hard-case. Dresses the part too. You know, cast-off Space Corps uniform, bandoliers, wide-brimmed tropical hat. You can't miss him.'

Fenner patted the butt of the laser-rifle cradled in his lap. 'I don't intend to!'

The hovercraft sped on.

As it disappeared in a cloud of spray, the reeds parted and two slender craft appeared. They were paddled by green-skinned Swampie warriors in leather loin-cloths, and they were piled high with sealed plastic crates.

In the prow of the second craft was a burly, sweating figure in a wrinkled tropical uniform with no insignia, and a broad-brimmed tropical hat. In the back was Romana. She was gagged and her arms were bound. The slender craft glided swiftly and silently across the main channel, and disappeared into one of the innumerable side-channels. The Swampies had their own ways of travelling, using tiny creeks that cut through the swamplands.

The Doctor played an experimental trill on his reed flute. He was vaguely worried. Romana should have been visible on the top of the little knoll by now. She was nowhere to be seen. He got up and headed towards the knoll.

Suddenly a hovercraft came roaring down the main channel. The Doctor waved sociably—and a laser-bolt whizzed past his head. He dived for cover, landing flat on his face in the reeds.

In the hovercraft, Fenner cursed, as the tall figure in the broad-brimmed hat disappeared from view. 'I think I hit him! Pull up, I'll go and check.'

Thawn drove the hovercraft up the bank. Fenner leaped out and went crashing into the reed-beds.

Nearby, Rohm Dutt signalled his paddlers to halt. 'That was a laser-rifle! What's going on?'

Beside him in the boat crouched Varlik, a muscular, young war-chief. 'We are near the Refinery. Perhaps one of the dryfoots is out hunting.' 'Dryfoot' was the Swampie term for anyone not one of themselves. It held strong overtones of contempt.

Rohm Dutt shook his head. 'That lot? They're technicians.' He pronounced the word with the same contempt Varlik gave to 'dryfoot'. 'Technicians don't hurt. They'd have to leave their computers behind. They're after *me*! Come on, let's get a move on now.'

The paddlers bent to their work, and the two craft sped on.

The Doctor was lying face-down in a clump of reeds, wondering if it was safe to move. He heard the sound of someone crashing towards him, turned his head and opened one cautious eye. An angry-looking man was standing over him with a laser-rifle. 'So much for Rohm Dutt. I never did like gun-runners.' The man raised the laser-rifle evidently determined to finish his victim off.

The Doctor tensed himself to roll aside. If the first shot missed, he could jump the man and . . .

A second voice yelled, 'Hold it Fenner! That's not Rohm Dutt.' A second man came running up. The first man turned on him angrily. 'What do you mean? Look at him, hat and everything. You described him yourself.'

'I tell you it isn't Rohm Dutt. I've seen him on Delta Magna plenty of times. You've shot the wrong man!'

The Doctor got to his feet. 'To be precise, you've shot the wrong man's hat.' He took off his hat, studied the laser-burn on the brim and looked reprovingly at the man with the rifle. 'Really, Fenner, fancy taking me for Rohm Dutt!'

The laser-rifle was still covering him. 'All right, then who are you?'

'Oh, just call me the Doctor.'

'What are you doing here?' demanded the second man.

'A sort of survey,' said the Doctor vaguely. 'At the moment I'm looking for my friend. By the way, who are you?'

'My name's Thawn, Refinery Controller. This is my assistant, Fenner.'

Suddenly the Doctor turned and marched off down the path, Thawn and Fenner trailing baffled behind him.

The Doctor reached the lower slopes of the knoll and studied the area around him with concern. 'It looks as if something must have happened to her. Look at the way these reeds are crushed. There was some kind of struggle ...' He noticed something glinting in the mud and picked it up. It was the Tracer. 'Something's happened to her or she'd never have dropped this.' He slipped the Tracer in his pocket.

'The Swampies must have got her,' said Thawn.

The Doctor looked up. 'Swampies? I take it those are the native inhabitants?'

Thawn nodded, and Fenner said uneasily. 'They don't usually come this close to the Refinery. Either they're getting bolder—or they had good reason.'

Thawn looked around the endlessly rustling reed-beds. 'There could be dozens of them in there. If they jump us here we won't stand a chance.'

'How do I get in touch with these Swampies?' asked the Doctor impatiently.

'Forget it. You're coming back to the Refinery with us.'

'Oh no I'm not, I'm looking for my friend. Sorry.'

Fenner raised his rifle. 'I'm afraid I must insist. You've still got a lot of questions to answer.'

'It would be uncivil to refuse such a gracious invitation,' said the Doctor politely. 'Any chance of strawberry jam for tea?'

After what felt like a longish journey Romana was lifted from the boat, carried a short distance and lashed to something heavy. The blindfold was taken from her eyes.

Blinking, she looked around her. She was inside a kind of stockade, a rough wooden fence enclosing an area of muddy ground. There were a number of reed huts inside the stockade and she was tied to a massive log just in front of the largest.

Surrounding her was a semi-circle of fierce-looking green-skinned warriors. A burly hard-faced man in sweat-stained clothes and broad-brimmed tropical hat pushed his way through the warriors, waving them away. He lowered himself wearily on to the log. 'You know, there's a thing called the drill-fly in these swamps. Lays its eggs in your feet, and a week later you get holes in your head.'

Romana glared at him. 'Just how long am I going to be kept tied up here?'

'Well now, that depends.'

'On what?'

'On whether you co-operate or not. If you do, I'll try to persuade them to let you go. If you don't, you'll stay there till you rot—and believe me, in this climate, it doesn't take long. Of course, the insects may get you first.'

'And that doesn't bother you?'

'Me?' The burly man laughed. 'I'm indifferent. I'm Rohm Dutt, young woman, maybe you've heard of me? I'm a gun-runner—and you're a Government spy.

The Swampies can do what they like with you.'

Romana looked severely at him. 'Emotional callousness is usually indicative of psychological trauma.'

'Yeah? To think I never knew that!' There was a distant roll of thunder. Rohm Dutt cocked his head. 'Never known such a place for rainstorms—that's why everything's so wet! Well, are you going to co-operate?'

'How?'

'By answering my questions. For a start, are you from the Refinery?'

'What Refinery?'

Rohm Dutt nodded. 'Good for you. I thought you were going to lie. They don't have any women working there.'

'Look, I don't know what you're talking about—I've never even heard of any Refinery.'

'Don't get excited, young woman. Plenty of time to dig out the truth.'

'I'm already telling you the truth. You obviously think I'm someone I'm not.'

Rohm Dutt ignored her protests. 'They send you here alone, or with a team?'

'Only the Doctor. And nobody sent me.'

Rohm Dutt grunted. 'Where's this Doctor now?'

'Looking for me, I expect.'

'What were you doing in the swamps?'

'Catching butterflies.'

'Oh, I like a joke!' said Rohm Dutt with weary patience.

'Good. I'll try and think of one.'

Rohm Dutt leaned forward menacingly. 'What were you doing in the swamp?'

'Look, you'd be none the wiser if I told you.'

'*What were you doing in the swamp?*'

The questions went on and on.

The hovercraft was moored to the Refinery platform and the Doctor was marched up a metal ladder, and into a machinery-filled room. It was dominated by an enormous pipe which ran clear across the room, and disappeared into the wall. A technician was checking a set of gauges; he looked up as they came in. 'You got him then?'

Thawn shook his head. 'This isn't Rohm Dutt, Harg.'

'Who is he?'

Fenner said, 'We don't know who he is. We found him in the prohibited zone.'

The Doctor looked at his charred hat brim. 'You really ought to put up a notice. "Trespassers will be shot." Something simple like that. Who's Rohm Dutt?'

'He's a gun-runner. You're sure you don't know him?'

'Positive. I'm a stranger here.'

Thawn resumed the questioning. 'What were you doing in the swamps?'

'I've already told you—I was looking for my friend.'

Thawn looked threateningly at him. 'Looking for your friend in a forbidden zone close to a classified project could get you into a lot of trouble.'

'What classified project?'

'You're standing in the middle of it!'

The Doctor looked around him. 'This? A simple methane-based catalysing protein refinery. Why should it be secret?'

Thawn drew in his breath. 'You admit it, then? You know what this place is for?'

'Well, it's obvious, isn't it? I've seen hundreds of them.'

'He's crazy,' said Harg flatly.

'This refinery is a pilot project,' said Fenner. 'The first one ever built.'

The Doctor sighed. 'That's the trouble with you colonists from Earth, you're always so insular. Now if you'd been to Binaca-Ananda, you'd have seen one in every town.'

'Are you claiming you're from outside this star system?' demanded Thawn incredulously.

'Yes.'

'Then how did you get here?'

'Well, as a matter of fact, I have my own transport.'

Harg scratched his head. 'I told you—he's crazy!'

'Will you stop saying that?' said the Doctor. He turned indignantly to Thawn. 'You heard him. He keeps saying I'm crazy. What gives him such insight into my mental processes, eh? Tell me that!'

From the look on Thawn's face, he agreed with Harg. 'You claim to be an expert on this type of installation, do you, Doctor?'

'I'm an expert on most things actually,' said the

Doctor modestly. 'Yes, I think I might claim a working knowledge.'

Thawn's hand pointed upwards. 'All right, *expert*—what's that?'

'It's an air-vent. Very useful too, sometimes.'

'No, not the vent—the piece of machinery just below it.'

The Doctor squinted upwards and frowned. 'Oh that?'

'Yes that!' Thawn shot a triumphant look at Harg, sure that he'd caught the Doctor out.

'That,' said the Doctor deliberately, 'is a simple funicular gas separator.'

Thawn pointed again, a little to one side. 'And that?'

'Well,' said the Doctor judiciously. 'That looks to me like a rather primitive enzyme recycler with an injection circuit feeding the bacterium bioplast.'

There was a stunned silence.

'From there,' continued the Doctor airily, 'I imagine the raw protein is centrifuged, before being freeze-dried and compressed for packaging.'

Absorbed in his own lecture, the Doctor started wandering about the pump room, hands in his pockets. 'Incidentally, I think you might render the process considerably more efficient if you inserted a plasmin catalyst *after* the bioplast circuit ...'

There was a stunned silence.

'A plasmin catalyst?' said Fenner unbelievingly.

'Yes, why not?'

Harg looked at Thawn. 'You remember, sir, that seminar, just before we left Delta Magna? Research have been working on it for years. It'll be the next development of the process. It took a team of top scientists five years to come up with the idea of a plasmin catalyst—and he throws it out as a casual afterthought! That's brilliant!'

'All right, so he's brilliant!' snarled Thawn.

'Thank you,' said the Doctor. 'Am I free to go now?'

'No!'

'Why not?'

'You still haven't told us what you were doing in the swamps.'

'Yes, I did. Just a sort of survey.' The Doctor headed for the door. 'Now if you'll excuse me, I really must go and find Romana.'

Fenner moved to bar his way. 'I wouldn't. If the Swampies have taken her to their Settlement, you'll never reach her. Those swamps are bottomless—and only the Swampies know the paths.'

'That's right,' said Thawn. 'And if you do get through the swamps, you'll probably end up with a Swampie spear in your back. The Swampies have killed two of my men already.'

'Why?'

Before Thawn could answer the Doctor's question, a voice boomed from a loudspeaker. 'Attention, attention. Orbit shot in ten minutes.'

'Orbit shot?' asked the Doctor curiously. 'What's that?'

31

'Why don't you come and see?' invited Thawn sardonically. 'We'll watch it from the control centre.'

Still fastened to her log, Romana watched Rohm Dutt prise the lid off a plastic crate and fish out a squat wide-barrelled rifle. He held it up to the admiring circle of warriors around him. 'There you are. Sixty-calibre gas-operated Stelsons. It's a simple weapon, you'll soon get the hang of them.'

A warrior in a cloak and an elaborate head-dress stepped forward. He was middle-aged, though still lean and tough, and he had the look of unquestioned authority. His name was Ranquin, and he was supreme chief of the tribe. Ranquin took the gun and examined it. He looked at the other guns in the crate. 'The guns are old.'

'Oh come on now, Chief, they need cleaning, true enough, they've been in storage a long time. But these guns have never been out of their crates. They're in perfect working order.'

Varlik, the war-chief came forward. 'Where are the magazines?'

Rohm Dutt pointed to a nearby crate. 'In there. Two for each gun.'

'And the spare ammunition?'

'You've got forty guns. That makes eighty magazines with fifty rounds in each. Is there an army at the Refinery?'

Ranquin laughed grimly. 'You are my brother,

Rohm Dutt. With the weapons you bring we shall drive the dryfoots from our sacred waters.'

'That is why the Sons of Earth sent them to you, Chief.' Rohm Dutt fished out a sheet of paper from inside his tunic. 'Now, if you'll just be kind enough to put your signature on this.'

Skart, the Chief's High Priest, said suspiciously, 'What is this signature?'

'Look, just make your mark, anything you like. It's just to say that I've made the delivery. I have to show them the paper back on Delta Magna.'

Ranquin looked ironically at him. 'Can it be that the Sons of Earth do not trust my brother?'

'It's just a matter of business, Chief, you know. Look, just make your mark, anything you like. Put your seal on it.'

Ranquin fingered the carved head of his staff. 'This bears the Sign of Kroll, it is sacred to our people.'

'That will do very nicely,' said Rohm Dutt hurriedly. He held out the paper. Skart produced a pot of thick black ink, and the Sign of Kroll, a squiggly octopus-like design, was duly affixed to the bottom of the paper.

'Thank you,' said Rohm Dutt, and stowed the paper away. It was clear to Romana that he was in a hurry to be off.

Ranquin nodded towards her. 'What of the dryfoot woman my men captured. Was she spying on us?'

'I think she must have been, Chief. But she's stubborn, she'll admit nothing.'

Skart moved closer to his Chief. 'Let us offer her to the Great One. Always in the past when our people went to battle, they first made a blood sacrifice to Kroll.'

Ranquin considered for a moment, then nodded decisively. 'So be it. We will use the dryfoot woman to ensure that we triumph over her fellows. She shall be sacrificed to Kroll!'

3

The Sacrifice

The Doctor's interest in the workings of the Refinery
was so obviously genuine that Thawn and the other
technicians found themselves explaining the entire
operation. The Doctor listened with flattering attention.

'The Refinery produces a hundred tons of compressed protein every day,' explained Thawn proudly.
'We package it in an unmanned cargo-rocket and shoot
it into orbit round Delta Magna, every twelve hours.
They collect the rockets and take them down to the
planetary surface.'

'That's what makes the operation viable,' said Fenner. 'If we had to use space freighters the costs would
be too high.'

'The planet is fully automated of course,' Thawn
went on. 'The computer controls the orbit shot, but I
always like to double-check. If there's a misfire, we
have a manual override.'

The Doctor watched a green-skinned figure bring
forward a tray full of drinks. 'You do all this with just
the five of you here?'

Thawn gave him a puzzled look. 'Four, Doctor.'

The Doctor looked round the room, counting. 'I make it five. One, two, three, four, five.'

Thawn laughed. 'Oh, I see. You were counting Mensch. He's only a Swampie.'

'So he doesn't count?' said the Doctor thoughtfully. 'Perhaps that's why his friends keep attacking you!'

'They attack us because they're ignorant savages.'

'They were the first on Delta Magna,' said Dugeen mildly. 'We took their planet away from them and sent them here. Now they're afraid we'll take what they've got left.'

Fenner looked curiously at him. 'Sometimes, Dugeen, I wonder if the Sons of Earth haven't been getting at you.'

Harg looked up from the controls. 'Two minutes to orbit shot.'

'Listen,' said Dugeen heatedly. 'When this plant is declared a success they'll put ten full-scale refineries on here. There'll be no room for the natives then—and they know it!'

The Doctor wandered over to a wall-map which showed the immense lake, almost an inland sea, which took up so much of the surface of Delta Three. 'Even a lake this size couldn't support *ten* full-scale refineries, surely?'

'Oh yes it can,' said Fenner positively.

'But the protein density of the lake would have to be colossal.'

'It is, Doctor.' Thawn said proudly. 'I discovered it

myself. I calculate that this lake can supply one fifth of the protein requirements for the whole of Delta Magna.'

'That's very impressive. Tell me, where were these two men of yours when they were killed?'

'Out on the lake, taking samples.'

'What happened to them? Exactly how were they killed?'

'They just vanished. We never found their bodies—the Swampies made sure of that.'

'Then surely it could have been an accident? Perhaps they just drowned?'

Thawn shook his head. '*Two* experienced men? No, Doctor, they were killed.'

'Thirty seconds to shot,' announced Harg.

'It could have been an accident,' insisted the Doctor. 'Or something else, some other danger you don't even know about. It hardly seems fair to blame the Swampies—particularly if you're just about to dispose of them for the second time.'

'Don't you worry about the Swampies,' said Thawn impatiently. 'The Government will take care of them —provided they see reason.'

The Doctor looked at the silent, green skinned figure in the corner. 'What will it do—teach them to carry trays, like our friend here?'

'Why not? Tell me, Doctor, would you let a small band of semi-savages stand in the way of progress?'

'Progress is a very flexible word—and it can mean

just about anything you want it to, depending on who's speaking.'

'Countdown!' announced Harg. 'Ten, nine, eight . . .'

'All external doors sealed,' ordered Thawn.

Dugeen said, 'Seven, six, five, four . . .'

The Doctor slipped away.

'Three, two, one, zero!'

A throbbing roar shook the Refinery as the cargo-rocket blasted off.

Another shipment of protein was on its way to feed the hungry millions on Delta Magna.

Soon after dark, Romana was taken to the Temple of Kroll, just outside the stockade. It was little more than a glorified log hut, its wooden gate-pillars carved with the Sign of Kroll. A huge metal gong hung beside the gates.

Romana was shackled to another log, just inside the temple doors. Beside her was a flat stone slab. Skart moved forward with a blazing torch, and great jets of swamp gas caught fire and flared high around her. She lay chained and helpless in the middle of a circle of flame, watched by an awe-struck group of warriors.

Romana lifted her head, and saw Rohm Dutt standing with the others, his face impassive. 'I suppose you're enjoying this,' she called.

'Makes no odds to me. I'll be on my way back to Delta Magna soon. Any last messages for your friends in Government Security?'

Before Romana could answer, Ranquin came forward. He was wearing his ceremonial cloak. 'All is ready in the Temple of Kroll.'

Skart bowed low. 'The offering is prepared.'

A distant explosion shook the ground beneath their feet, and rumbled away over the marshes.

Rohm Dutt looked up at the sky. A fiery streak was disappearing from view. 'Another orbit shot?'

Varlik nodded. 'Soon there will be no more such blasphemies!'

Ranquin raised his voice in a ritual chant. 'Open the pit. Let Kroll be summoned from the depths!'

A group of sweating warriors rolled away the slab, and Romana twisted her head, staring down into blackness.

Ranquin took up a metal hammer and struck three times upon the gong. The brazen clangour of the gong-notes echoed across the swamplands. From inside the stockade came the steady beat of drums.

Ranquin chanted, 'O Kroll, hear thy people. We summon thee, O Kroll! We offer this girl's life in tribute to thy greatness. Guide and protect us O Great One. Give victory to thy people, in the struggle that lies ahead.'

He struck the gong again, and turned and led the warriors away, back inside the stockade.

Rohm Dutt lingered a moment, then followed the others. Romana was left alone, surrounded by the fiercely-blazing gas jets, staring down into the darkness of the pit.

The Doctor was wandering around the pump rooms, studying the dials and pressure gauges when Thawn appeared.

'Ah, there you are, Doctor. We were wondering what had become of you.'

'Oh I just thought I'd poke around a bit. When you've seen one orbit shot you've seen 'em all! What's that noise?'

Thawn listened. A steady drum-beat was rolling across the swamplands. 'It's coming from the direction of the Settlement.'

'Maybe they're having a dance,' said the Doctor lightly, but his face was grave.

Suddenly Mensch spoke from the doorway. 'My people summon Kroll. They are making a blood sacrifice.'

'Who's Kroll?'

'It's the Swampie name for a kind of giant squid,' said Thawn. 'Centuries ago when we resettled the Swampies here, we shipped along a couple of specimens and turned them loose in the swamp, just to keep the Swampies happy.'

'A blood sacrifice,' said the Doctor slowly. 'I don't like the sound of that at all. I think I'd better go and find my friend now.'

'Don't be stupid, Doctor. You'll never cross those swamps on your own.'

'In most primitive cultures it's common to sacrifice an enemy—a stranger. I've got a shrewd idea who that stranger might be. Romana can be a difficult guest!'

'Wait till it gets light at least. We'll take the hover-craft, and go in force.'

'Why are you so keen to help me all of a sudden?'

'You heard what Mensch said. If the Swampies *are* holding a blood sacrifice, they're preparing for war. And that means Rohm Dutt got through with those guns. We've got enough weapons here to knock out that settlement in a couple of minutes. Now the Swampies are armed, we've *got* to strike first, in self-defence.'

The Doctor shook his head, 'I'm planning a rescue, not a massacre. I'll go alone, as soon as it gets light. Now I must get some sleep.' The Doctor slipped away.

Thawn turned and hurried back to control. Mensch, ignored as usual, was left alone in the pump room. As soon as Thawn was out of sight, Mensch hurried to a bank of machinery, groped beneath it, and produced a primitive lantern. Lighting it with flint and steel from a belt pouch, he hurried to the window and slid back the shutter. He began signalling with the lantern, opening and closing it to produce an irregular flashing.

The Doctor watched thoughtfully from just outside the door, pleased to have his theory confirmed.

Since by all accounts the Swampies were a fierce, war-like people, why should one of them come to act as a servant at the hated Refinery? Surely only in order to spy upon the enemy.

Now Mensch was reporting Thawn's planned attack to his people. But how? Surely the lantern-flash would not carry all the way to the Settlement?

Suddenly the Doctor saw a light over Mensch's shoulder, flashing a reply from somewhere in the swamp. One of Mensch's fellow tribesmen, no doubt posted in the swamplands nearby, acting as a kind of courier. Soon he would be taking Mensch's message back to his people.

It occurred to the Doctor that the courier might serve as a guide.

He hurried out into the darkness of the Refinery platform, and stood looking around him in the dank warm tropical night. There, not far away, the light was still flashing. The Doctor climbed down a steel ladder. A swampie canoe was moored at the bottom, and the Doctor climbed into it.

The tribesman stood on the mound overlooking the Refinery, absorbing the message that Mensch was sending. When the message was complete, he flashed acknowledgement and moved away to the stream. He climbed into a hidden canoe and paddled away in the direction of the Settlement.

Seconds later, the Doctor's boat moved silently down the stream, following the messenger.

Straining her eyes, Romana peered into the mouth of the pit. Was something moving down there in the blackness? It was hard to see clearly in the fitful glare of the gas-jets. 'It's all nonsense,' she muttered to herself uneasily. 'Primitive spirit worship!' An eerie whistling sound came from the pit ...

The sound could be heard, though faintly, by the little knot of warriors waiting inside the entrance to the stockade.

Ranquin looked around the circle of rapt, intense faces. 'Kroll rises,' he whispered. 'Kroll rises from the depths!'

The whistling, gurgling sound was louder now.

Romana strained her eyes.

Something *was* coming out of the pit.

It was a wriggling, heaving, shapeless glob, faintly luminous in the darkness.

As she watched, it reached out a long tentacle, ending in a huge snapping claw.

Claw snapping, the tentacle shot out of the pit towards her ...

Romana screamed.

4

The Tunnel

Romana screamed and twisted in her chains, but it was no use. It was almost as if her screams guided the long tentacle towards her. It came closer, closer ... then swooped forward. The claw clamped round her neck, choking her.

She struggled wildly, but the claw tightened its grip remorselessly, crushing the breath from her throat.

Suddenly the Doctor bounded out of the darkness, snatched up the heavy metal gong-striker and smashed it down on the shapeless body of the monster. There was a thud and a grunt, and the claw went slack, dropping away from Romana's throat.

The Doctor grabbed the tentacle and heaved, pulling the monster bodily out of the pit. But what emerged wasn't a monster at all. It was the Swampie High Priest, wrapped in a bundle of luminous skins. The tentacle was a long skin-covered pole. Presumably there were some kind of tongs to work the snapper claw. It all looked incredibly crude, and primitive: Romana was disgusted with herself for being so terrified by such a simple device.

The Doctor smiled, guessing what she was feeling.

'Never mind, Romana. He probably looked a lot more convincing from the front.'

'Only too convincing! How did you know it was a fake?'

The Doctor pointed to a line of wet footprints leading from the edge of the pit.

'There's no need to be so smug about it, Doctor!'

'I'm not being smug.'

'Oh yes you are! I can tell that expression, even from behind.'

The Doctor went over to the altar, and studied it carefully. 'You may have had a lucky escape after all Romana. There was a Kroll once, a real one.'

'How do you know?'

'There are real sucker marks here, huge ones. They're actually gouged deep into the stone. Pretty ancient though, judging by the way the serrations have eroded.'

Romana shuddered, visualising a creature so huge and powerful that it could leave its mark on stone, 'Presumably that must have been Kroll—the real Kroll.'

'They told you about their local water deity?'

'Oh yes! They seemed to think I should be honoured to be sacrificed to him.'

'Sacrificed to his memory, more like it,' said the Doctor thoughtfully. 'The real Kroll was brought from Delta Magna hundreds of years ago. Surely he must be dead by now.'

Romana said, 'That explains the masquerade. The

priests must have started to fake the monster just to inspire the faithful. It's all political, really.'

'Don't talk to me about politics,' muttered the Doctor. He bent to examine the crude padlock on the chains holding Romana to the log.

Romana looked over his shoulder and her eyes widened. The bundle of skins in the corner was moving. 'Look out, Doctor!'

The Doctor whirled round, ducked—and the heavy ceremonial knife clattered harmlessly off the altar.

The Doctor jumped forward, but the priest was already disappearing into the darkness.

The Doctor knelt beside Romana, fished out a picklock from his pocket, and set to work on the padlock. 'I think we'd better get you away from here.'

'It would be nice,' agreed Romana faintly.

'I wonder where they found this padlock. Brought it from Delta Magna probably. It's a real antique.'

'Fascinating!' Romana hesitated. 'Doctor, there's something I have to tell you.'

'What?'

'When they captured me—I dropped the Tracer.'

The Doctor patted his pocket. 'That's all right. I picked it up again.'

'Then as soon as you can get me out of here, we can go and hunt for the fifth segment.'

'Not till it gets light, we can't. It would be extremely foolhardy to go wandering around that swamp in the dark.'

There was a click and the padlock sprang open.

Romana struggled free of the heavy chains. 'We can't stay here, Doctor. Our Monster friend will be back any minute with his warriors.'

'I doubt it,' said the Doctor cheerfully. 'He's got to keep this business about the fake pretty quiet, remember. Very embarrassing if the congregation found out the truth. Besides, the warriors will all be busy digging trenches. They expect to be attacked at any moment. I followed a Swampie messenger who was carrying information.'

'How did you manage that?'

'Oh, it wasn't too difficult,' said the Doctor airily. 'Thawn, the Refinery boss, was keen on organising a massacre, so I just slipped away.'

Romana stretched her arms and legs, stiff and aching after her long captivity. 'What is this Refinery? They seemed to think I might have come from it originally.'

'It's a primitive methane catalysing protein refinery. A pilot plant for bigger things apparently. You see the people of Delta Magna—which was originally an Earth colony by the way—shipped our green friends up here when they colonised the planet.'

'Presumably because they thought this moon was no use to anybody?'

'That's right. But now they're discovered there may be something they want here after all.'

'What something?'

'Protein,' said the Doctor. 'Protein, refined from this enormous lake. I wouldn't have thought there was

47

enough here to make it worthwhile, but they're already producing a hundred tons of compressed protein twice a day, and they estimate they can get ten times more than that.'

Romana did a few rapid mental calculations. 'But that's ridiculous. How could the lake produce that much protein? Where's it coming from?'

'That's something I haven't discovered yet. But it's obviously produced by something, somehow. And in big enough quantities to make it worth fighting over.'

Romana thought of the savage green-skinned warriors who had been her captors. 'This lot are spoiling for a war as well. They've got arms now. There's a gun-runner here called Rohm Dutt. He thought I was a spy trying to get evidence against him.' She looked at the altar. 'The whole idea of my being sacrificed was to propitiate Kroll, get him on their side in the coming battle.'

As always, the Doctor was unable to resist a puzzle. 'Rohm Dutt eh? So Thawn was right. But who's paying Rohm Dutt for his trouble? These people obviously don't use money. And how come Thawn seemed to know so much about him?'

Romana sighed. 'Does it matter, Doctor? It'll be light soon. Let's just find the segment and leave them to their war.'

The Doctor was looking thoughtfully into the pit. 'I wonder what they keep down there—besides fake monsters?'

Rohm Dutt awoke from a nightmare in which he was being chased by hordes of green warriors, straight into the tentacles of a giant squid. He awoke to find a green face hovering over him. At first he thought it was part of his nightmare, and then realised that he was on his bed in the guest hut, inside the Swampie stockade. Varlik was shaking him awake. Ranquin the Swampie chief looked on impassively.

Rohm Dutt shook his aching head, and struggled up on to one elbow. 'What is it?'

'We have had a message from Mensch, the one who watches our enemies at the Refinery. The dryfoots plan to attack us at dawn.'

Rohm Dutt was baffled. 'What? Them attack you? Here, at the Settlement? That wasn't what was——' He broke off, shaking his head in confusion.

'They are coming in their air-boats at dawn,' said Ranquin.

Rohm Dutt struggled to his feet. 'You must lead your people away from here at once, Chief. Take them to hide in the swamps, they'll never find you there.'

To Rohm Dutt's horror, Ranquin shook his head. 'We shall not run from the dryfoots, ever again. We have weapons now.'

'But you don't know how to use them!'

Varlik slapped the magazine of the rifle tucked under his arm. 'You said yourself, the rifle is not a difficult weapon.'

'You still have to know one end from the other!'

'You are like all dryfoots! Yau think because we

49

lead a simple life that we must be fools. My men are warriors!'

'I know, I know,' said Rohm Dutt placatingly. 'All I'm saying is, you're not *ready* to fight yet. If you split into small groups and spread out across the swamps they'll never be able to hit you.'

Ranquin shook his head. 'Our battle plan is already made. We shall ambush them when they are in the open, upon the lake. They are only a handful. We shall take them by surprise.'

Rohm Dutt changed his tack. 'Chief, even if you succeed this time, that won't be the end of it. Others will come to avenge them.'

Ranquin's voice was shaking with anger. 'They are aggressors, invaders of our waters. They have no right here. Are there not many on Delta Magna itself who support our cause? Why else would the Sons of Earth send us these weapons?'

Rohm Dutt's massive shoulders slumped dejectedly. 'Have it your way. I still say it's too early to fight them.'

Ranquin looked shrewdly at him. 'I think you would rather we waited until you were safely back on Delta Magna, Rohm Dutt.'

'Sure, why not? I came here to supply you with arms, not to watch you use them.'

Varlik's green hand fell like a clamp on Rohm Dutt's meaty shoulder. 'But you will fight with us to-morrow, *brother*. We shall need every gun!'

Rohm Dutt was too terrified to reply.

Ranquin smiled contemptuously, and left the hut. Varlik followed him.

Rohm Dutt sank back on his bed, glaring angrily after them. He knew they thought he was a coward—but they were wrong. Rohm Dutt had been in a score of pitched battles up and down the entire star system. Fights with rival gun-runners and smugglers, battles with Government Police craft. In the normal way he didn't mind a fight, enjoyed it even. But this was different.

Rohm Dutt had good reason to fear tomorrow's battle.

Like the Swampies, he had very little chance of coming out of it alive.

He lay back on his straw bed, sweating with fear, dreading the dawn.

5

The Thing in the Lake

There might be a battle planned for tomorrow, but the routine work of the Refinery had to go on as usual.

In the control room, Dugeen was studying the screen of a radar scanner. It covered the whole of the immense lagoon, charting its shifting currents and the movements of the muddy bed. He looked up at Thawn. 'You see? Look, I've been recording these scans every five minutes.'

Something very odd indeed was showing up on the scanner—a massive disturbance in the centre of the lagoon.

Thawn frowned at the screen. 'What's the latest picture?'

'Coming up.' Dugeen clicked a control and the picture changed slightly.

'That's weird ... it's as if something's lifted up the centre of the lagoon bed, and then settled back again. Could it be a gas build-up?'

'I doubt it sir, not over that area.'

'We'd better sink probes in the centre there, take a few samples. We've got to find out what's going on.'

Fenner came into the room. 'That Doctor chap seems to have disappeared.'

'Have you looked in the sleeping quarters? He said he was going to get some sleep.'

'Of course I've looked in the sleeping quarters,' snapped Fenner irritably. 'I've looked everywhere, searched the Refinery. He's gone—and Mensch says one of the boats is missing.'

Dugeen looked up from his screen. 'I know this is a bit wild, sir, but do you think he could be connected with this business here?' He indicated the mysterious trace on the screen. 'I mean it only showed up after he arrived.'

Fenner went over to the screen. 'What's going on?'

'This!' said Thawn pointing to the mysterious trace-pattern. 'Have you ever seen anything like it before?'

Fenner studied the screen. 'No, I haven't. But surely whatever it is, it's enormous. I doubt if our mystery friend could be responsible for anything on that scale, not on his own.'

Thawn stroked his moustache. 'Then maybe he's not on his own. He was talking about a missing friend when we picked him up, remember?'

'Well, maybe he's got more than one friend on Delta Three,' said Dugeen. 'We don't even know how he got here.'

'Or how long he's been here,' said Thawn slowly. 'We're assuming he couldn't have done much harm because he was here with us. But suppose he came to

53

Delta Three some time ago? Suppose he's got friends hiding out there in the swamps?'

Fenner gave him a puzzled look. 'It's possible, I suppose ... But what are they up to?'

'That's obvious, surely. They're trying to sabotage the work of this Refinery.' He jerked a thumb at the radar screen. 'All that could be part of it. They're carrying out some kind of activity on the lake bed, trying to contaminate the protein source. This Doctor is a scientist of some kind. Look how much he seemed to know about this place.' Thawn paused, considering. 'Of course, that could all have been an act. Maybe he was just very well briefed.'

Fenner shook his head. 'No, no, he's a scientist all right. You remember that business about the plasmin catalyst? He couldn't have faked all that.'

'Well, whoever he is, I reckon he's come here to help the Swampies. You say there's a boat missing?' Fenner nodded, and Thawn went on, 'Well, if he took a boat rather than a hovercraft ... it means he didn't want the noise of an engine. He wanted to contact them secretly.'

'Why would he risk trying to cross the swamp, alone and at night?'

'Because he's a Swampie lover. It isn't a risk at all for him. He's in with them!'

'You think he's gone to warn them we're coming?'

Thawn pounded a fist into the palm of his hand. 'Exactly! I had an instinct about him from the very beginning. He was too glib by half. He's one of them all right, one of those fanatics from the Sons of Earth. I'm going to take Mensch for a guide, and go after him in one of the hovercraft.'

Fenner looked thoughtfully at him. 'I wouldn't bother. He'll have to leave the boat eventually, and if he wanders off the path—well, the Sons of Earth won't be much help to him then. He'll probably be dead by morning.'

Thawn took a laser rifle from a rack on the wall. 'Oh, he will, Fenner, he will. I intend to make quite certain of it!'

The Doctor climbed out of the tunnel with a massive leather-bound volume under his arm. 'There's a kind of secret room, full of religious relics. I found this.'

'What is it?'

The Doctor opened the book. Its pages were filled with drawings of tiny figures, lines of blurred writing underneath. 'I think it's a kind of illustrated history of the tribe. The Bayeux Tapestry—with footnotes!'

Romana looked over his shoulder. 'A sort of Holy Writ?'

The Doctor peered at the cramped writing. 'I think it's atrociously writ, actually. But the pictures aren't bad. Look, this sequence shows them being evicted from Delta Magna. They were given this moon as a sort of reservation ... There's Kroll.' The Doctor pointed to another drawing. A tiny priest-like figure stood before an altar, holding a shining object high in front of him. An enormous octopoid shape loomed behind the altar, towering over him.

'What does the writing say?'

'Let me see.' The Doctor began to read. ' "And when Kroll awakened, he saw that the people were fat and indolent. And then Kroll became angry and struck them down, swallowing into himself the symbol of his power and killing all who were in the Temple, even unto Hajes the High Priest. Great was the lamentation of the people. But Kroll returned to the water and slept, and would not hear them." '

Romana shivered. 'I prefer a book with a happy ending!'

' "Thus was the third manifestation of Kroll!" ' The Doctor closed the book. 'Well, you can say one thing for Kroll, he's obviously not one of those monsters who's always hanging about the place.'

'Just pops up every few hundred years, is that it?'

The Doctor nodded. 'A dormancy period of that length usually indicates a creature of enormous size . . .'

'You think Kroll really exists?'

The Doctor nodded gravely. 'Yes I do. I think Kroll is probably still around—and just about due for his fourth manifestation!'

Romana jumped up. 'Then let's not stay here and wait for it!' She looked outside the temple. 'It's nearly light now, Doctor. Can't we get away from here.'

The Doctor yawned, and stretched. 'Right as always, Romana. Time we were on our way. I've got a boat hidden in the marshes . . .'

They crept cautiously out of the Temple.

The ambush was prepared.

To reach the Settlement, the technicians from the Refinery had to use the main water-ways—the sub-channels were too small for their hovercraft.

At a kind of bottleneck, a point where the channel was narrowest and the reeds thickest, the Swampies lay in ambush.

Many of the warriors clutched one of the new Stelson rifles. The rest had spears, and knives.

Everything was ready.

Rohm Dutt watched the preparations with gloomy anticipation. The Swampie warrior beside him was studying the mechanism of his rifle in child-like fascination, thrusting the muzzle almost under Rohm Dutt's chin. The gun-runner struck the barrel aside. 'That way you fool. Don't point it at me!'

In a clump of reeds overlooking the main channel, Ranquin the Chief was having an agitated conference with Skart, his High Priest.

'Where did this stranger come from?'

'I do not know. He struck me down from behind.'

'So the sacrifice was not made,' whispered Ranquin. 'You did well to keep silence until we were alone, Skart. No one must know of this. They would think it a bad omen.'

A cunning gleam came into Skart's eyes. 'But the dryfoot woman will be gone. We can say Kroll took her.'

'Then there must be fresh blood on the altar stone for the faithful to see.'

'There will be,' promised Skart. 'I will see to it when we return. Trust me.'

He slipped away.

Thawn and Mensch roared down-stream in the Refinery hovercraft. Suddenly Mensch pointed.

The Doctor's abandoned skiff was drawn up at the bank, tied to a knotted tree-root.

Thawn swung the hovercraft towards the bank.

In the reeds Varlik held up his hand to restrain his warriors. 'Wait—do not fire. There is only one airboat. There must be others.'

The hovercraft glided up the bank, and Mensch jumped out to examine the boat.

Thawn was at the wheel of the hovercraft, clearly visible from the reed-beds.

The Swampie warrior next to Rohm Dutt could wait no longer. The glory of killing the enemy chief was too great to resist. He took careful aim at the figure in the hovercraft and pulled the trigger.

The gun exploded blowing away most of the warrior's head.

A second later, an immense, many-suckered tentacle slid out of the lake, curled round Mensch, and dragged him screaming into the water.

Rohm Dutt jumped to his feet and raced down the bank, towards the hovercraft. 'Thawn, wait! It's me, Rohm Dutt!'

Something unbelievable rose out of the water in front of him.

It was so huge, so horrible, so terrifying that the eye and the mind could scarcely take it in. An immense octopus-like shape towering mountain-like above the flat swamplands. Rohm Dutt gave a yell of pure terror, and turned and fled.

Thawn threw the hovercraft into gear, spun it round and roared away over the horizon.

Ranquin however, walked towards the incredible shape, his face lit up with ecstasy. 'It is Kroll, Varlik. See it is Kroll. O Kroll, Great One, spare thy true servants.'

Varlik, less religiously minded and more practical, threw himself at the Chief's knees, bringing him down into the shelter of the reeds.

Kroll gave a terrifying, whistling roar and disappeared below the lagoon.

Ranquin struggled to his feet, his face ecstatic. 'Kroll rose from the deep to protect his people. Let us give thanks to Kroll.'

The Swampie warriors fell to their knees. 'Praise to Kroll. Let us give praise to Kroll!'

Only Varlik did not join in the chant. He had picked up the rifle that had killed the warrior, and was examining the exploded magazine. 'First let us find Rohm Dutt, our brother. I think we have a score to settle with him.'

The warriors rose and began their search. No one could escape them for long in their native swamps.

The capture of Rohm Dutt was only a matter of time.

6

The Attack

Thawn lay slumped in a chair in the control room, and swigged down a beaker of brandy.

'Feeling better?' asked Fenner. 'What happened then? Was Mensch killed?'

'I think so, I didn't stay to watch.' He rubbed his hands over his eyes. 'The size of that thing. The sheer size ... It was unbelievable.'

Harg shook his head wonderingly. 'If it's as big as you say it is, how come we haven't spotted it before?'

'What about the Doctor?' asked Fenner. 'Did you see him?'

'No. But the Swampies *knew* we were coming. They were waiting in ambush, he must have warned them. They were armed too, one of them shot at me. Rohm Dutt was with them, they're all in it together. Maybe they came in on the same ship. The Sons of Earth have got to be the ones behind them. No one else has the resources for an operation like this—or the motive either.'

Harg was beginning to feel frightened. 'Shouldn't we send for reinforcements? A Government Security Unit?'

'No!' said Thawn fiercely. 'The Government are too soft. We must handle this ourselves. We'll do it my way.'

Fenner gave him a sceptical look. 'And what is your way?'

'We get rid of the problem once and for all.'

Fenner said slowly, 'If you're talking about mass murder, I won't agree to it.'

'It's the only way.'

'What about the creature you saw?' asked Harg.

Thawn swung round angrily. 'Obviously, we've got to deal with that too. We know it's lurking out there. Once we've located it, we can dispose of it with depth charges.'

Fenner moved over to the controls. 'I'll check the scanner.' He touched a control then stared at the screen in puzzlement. It showed only a blurred and fuzzy darkness. 'Nothing's registering. Maybe the scanner's defective.'

'Where's Dugeen?'

Harg checked a roster. 'In his quarters sir, it's his rest period.'

'Well get him down here, quick. He's supposed to be the radar expert isn't he?'

Harg spoke into the communicator. 'Dugeen, are you there? We need you in control.'

After a moment, a sleepy voice said, 'Dugeen here. You mean *now*?'

Thawn leaned over the mike. 'Now, Dugeen!'

'On my way, sir.'

Fenner flicked a control, with no appreciable result. 'That's scanner twelve, it's on the same parallel. I'll try fourteen.' He tried. The picture remained dark. 'We seem to have a signal, but no image.'

Dugeen came into control. His hair was tousled and he was rubbing his eyes. 'What's the problem?'

'Scanners twelve and fourteen,' said Fenner. 'They won't give any picture.'

Dugeen sat at the radar console and checked over the controls. 'Well, they're still functioning perfectly.'

'Then why aren't we getting any images?'

Dugeen looked up. 'Because there's something down there. Something so enormous it's blotting them out. I'll try long-range.'

A new image appeared, a kind of giant hump taking up the centre of the screen. It might have been an underwater mountain—or an octopus-like creature of unimaginable size.

Fenner looked at Dugeen. 'Well—what do you make of it?'

'Whatever it is, it's blotting out those other scanners. It could be a mass of sediment, thrown up when the lake bed moved ...'

Thawn was staring at the screen in horrified fascination. 'That's it! That's the thing I saw!'

'Those scanners are hundreds of yards apart,' said Fenner. 'Do you know how big that thing would have to be to blot them out?'

Thawn said fiercely. 'I saw it, I tell you. It's down there at the bottom of the lake—and it's alive!'

The Doctor was leading Romana through the swamps. 'I told them they had their figures wrong straight away. But of course, I didn't know about Kroll then ...'

Romana was exhausted after a sleepless night, followed by what seemed like hours squelching along muddy paths through featureless swamp. 'What are you talking about, Doctor?'

'The Refinery of course. You see, there can't possibly be enough living sediment in that lake, big as it is, to produce the amount of protein they're getting now, let alone what they hope to get. So—where's it coming from?'

'Kroll,' said Romana promptly. 'When a thing that size takes a nap for a couple of centuries, its feeding processes continue independently. Through its tentacles, probably.'

The Doctor was a little disappointed that Romana had already worked out the answer for herself. 'Thawn's men vanished while they were taking samples, drilling into the sediment at the bottom of the lake.'

'Just like prodding a sleeping tiger with a very sharp stick!' said Romana.

'That's right. And of course, the Refinery's heat exchangers must have raised the lake temperature several degrees. Then the noise of the orbit shots started rousing Kroll.'

'Doctor,' said Romana warningly.

The Doctor halted his lecture. 'What is it?'

'We've got company.'

Green-skinned warriors had appeared from the reed-beds, spears in their hands.

'I take it these are your friends, Romana,' said the Doctor brightly. 'Hadn't you better introduce me?'

'As what?'

'Oh, I don't know. Just as a wise and wonderful person who's come to solve all their problems. No need to exaggerate.'

Romana didn't think the Doctor's scheme would work, but she felt obliged to give it a try.

'This is the Doctor,' she began. 'He's ...'

'Seize them,' snarled Ranquin.

Warriors leaped upon the Doctor and Romana, binding their hands with grass ropes.

'I told you not to exaggerate,' said the Doctor reprovingly.

The Swampies dragged them away. They were taken back to the stockade, and tied to heavy logs in front of the chief's hut. Someone was already tied up there, a burly dishevelled figure, bleeding from a bruise on the forehead.

'Who's that?' asked the Doctor curiously.

'Rohm Dutt—a popular figure in these parts not long ago. It think he must have offended our hosts.'

Skart, the High Priest, smiled menacingly at Romana. 'Soon, dryfoot, you will wish you had died on the stone of blood.'

Ranquin turned to Varlik. 'Guard the dryfoots well. See no harm comes to them. I go to the temple to speak with Kroll. He will tell me by which of the Seven Holy Rituals they must meet their deaths.'

Thawn and Fenner were pacing up and down the control room, discussing ways of dealing with the colossal menace in the bottom of the lagoon. They weren't getting very far.

'Even depth charges aren't going to make much impression on a thing that size,' argued Fenner worriedly. 'Not unless we hit a vital spot first go—and there's no way of guaranteeing that.'

'We've got nothing else,' growled Thawn. '*You* think of a better way of killing it.'

'Why attack it at all? You know how long we've been operating here. This is the first we've seen of it. Surely if the thing were hostile we'd have known about it before? Why don't we just leave it alone, and hope it'll do the same for us?'

'Listen, Fenner, I've seen it, and you haven't. Believe me, it's hostile!' Thawn shuddered at the memory of the giant horror rising out of the swamp.

'All right, all right! All I'm saying is, depth charges will only provoke it.'

Dugeen looked up from his radar screen. 'Director. The thing seems to be on the move.'

They hurried over to the screen. The octopus-like hump was sidling slowly, very slowly, across the screen.

'Is it coming towards us?' asked Fenner.

'Difficult to say. It's coming closer certainly, but

66

not directly towards us, not yet. Look, it's stopped again.'

'Perhaps that's how it feeds,' suggested Fenner. 'It seems to be browsing across the bottom of the lake.'

'I'm not interested in its feeding habits, Fenner,' growled Thawn. 'Not unless it tries to extend them to us!'

'No, but listen. It lives and feeds in the water. Maybe we could poison it, saturate the area with cobalt, kill it with the radiation. Mind you, at that size it would need a massive dose.'

'Which would contaminate our protein source for a very long time,' Thawn pointed out. 'I still favour depth charges—I'll go and see how many we've got.'

He hurried out. Fenner watched him go despairingly. 'Depth charges! Like sticking pins in it.' He looked gloomily at the enormous humped shape on the screen. 'Take it from me, if Thawn attacks that thing with depth charges, he'll get us all killed.'

The Doctor and Romana waited, bound to the log. Varlik stood guard with a squad of spear-carrying warriors.

'I didn't like the bit about death according to one of the Seven Holy Rituals,' whispered Romana. 'What do you think they meant?'

'Oh, just the usual stuff,' said the Doctor carelessly. 'Fire, water, hanging upside down over a pit of vipers ...'

Romana shuddered. 'That's only three.'

'Well, use your imagination.'

'No thank you, I prefer not to!'

Rohm Dutt was recovering consciousness. He stared confusedly about him, then caught sight of Varlik. 'Help me!' he called weakly. 'Varlik—help me!'

Varlik strode over to him. 'Help *you*—traitor?'

'No, listen, Varlik, we're friends you and I. I've got money, Varlik, a lot of money, back on Delta Magna . . .'

Varlik looked scornfully at him. 'It is greed that has brought you to this, Rohm Dutt. You have betrayed the People of the Lakes. You brought us weapons that were old and rotten.'

'No, no,' protested Rohm Dutt feverishly. 'I told you they'd been in storage a long time. They need to be cleaned, that's all.'

'We have examined all your weapons, Rohm Dutt. The barrels are out of true, the metal of the magazines corroded, the ammunition defective. You thought you would be safely away from here before we tried to use them . . .'

'That isn't true. I bought the weapons in good faith. If they are defective then *I* was cheated. I'll get you better ones. Let me talk to Ranquin, let me explain . . .'

Varlik was implacable. 'There is nothing to be explained. We heard you call out to Thawn, leader of the dryfoots.'

'I was confused, Varlik. I was terrified. Seeing Kroll like that . . .'

'Will you never learn? We are simple people, savages if you like, but we are not fools. It was a plot. You brought us useless weapons so that we would enter into a battle we could not win. You cheated us, just as the dryfoots have always cheated our people.'

Rohm Dutt began babbling more excuses and explanations.

'It's no good,' said the Doctor. 'History is against you—quite apart from the fact that you're lying anyway.'

'What do you know about it?' snarled Rohm Dutt.

'I know a rogue when I see one. I've no desire to die in the company of a rogue, have you, Romana?'

'I've no desire to die at all, actually.'

The Doctor grinned sympathetically. 'How well I know that feeling! Look out, here comes the verdict!'

Ranquin strode towards them, Skart at his side. 'I have communed with the Great One in the Temple. He condemns the prisoners to die by the Seventh Holy Ritual of the Old Book.'

'Seven's my lucky number,' said the Doctor cheerfully.

Ranquin raised his hand. 'Let them be taken to the place of execution.'

Warriors surrounded the log, cutting the prisoners free, and seizing their arms.

'Ranquin, please, please, wait,' shouted Rohm Dutt.

'You're wasting your breath,' said the Doctor.

Romana dug in her heels, forcing her guards to

come to a halt in front of the chief. 'I demand to know why we're being sacrificed.'

Ranquin pointed to the Doctor. 'This one knows what he has done. He aroused the wrath of the Great One, by denying him his promised victim.'

The Doctor nodded towards Skart. 'He's not a Great One, he's an insignificant one. If you're going to have someone impersonate Kroll, you might try and be a bit more convincing.'

Ranquin moved closer, lowering his voice. 'When the servants of Kroll appear in his guise, they are as part of him, doing his bidding.'

'Nonsense,' said Romana spiritedly. 'All you're doing is keeping alive a myth. None of you here have ever even seen Kroll. You weren't even born at the time of the third manifestation.'

'You are wrong, dryfoot,' hissed Ranquin triumphantly. 'Kroll rose before us at dawn this very day. We were waiting to attack the dryfoots when Kroll appeared, and drove them away.' He raised his voice. 'Take them to the place of execution!'

As they were dragged towards the Temple the Doctor whispered, 'Kroll's on the move again already, Romana. There's even less time than I thought!'

Dugeen sat hunched over the scanner, watching the sinister humped outline on the screen. Fenner hovered worriedly over him. 'It hasn't moved for a good fifteen minutes.'

'There seems to be a bit of movement on the edge, a sort of regular rise and fall. Could be its breathing organs, I suppose.' Suddenly he broke off. 'Look, it's moving again. Coming straight towards us.'

Harg was checking the intake readings in the pump room when he heard a sound.

It was a kind of rumbling vibration, and it seemed to be running through the main access pipe. He paused, listening. The sound came again.

The pipe burst open, and an enormous grey tentacle flailed into the pump room.

In the control room, Dugeen and Fenner heard a distant scream. 'The pump room,' shouted Fenner. 'Come on.'

They ran out of the room and along the steel corridors of the Refinery.

At the door of the pump room they stopped frozen in unbelieving horror.

An enormous tentacle had wrapped itself around Harg's waist. It was dragging him towards the gap in the access pipe. With one last dreadful scream, Harg disappeared into the pipe.

7

The End of Harg

Fenner snatched a laser rifle from the wall rack and began blazing away. But it was too late. The giant tentacle had disappeared—taking Harg with it.

Thawn came running into the pump room. 'What's going on?'

'Quickly,' screamed Fenner. 'Shut down the main flow valve.'

The two men wrestled with the controls, spinning wheels and pulling levers, until at last the throbbing of the intake pump died away.

Thawn stared in horror at the shattered pipe. 'What's happened in here?'

Fenner leaned against the control bank gasping for breath. 'Harg has just been snatched out of here by that monster. One of its tentacles was right inside the main pipeline. He was in here running a check— then we heard him scream ...' Fenner broke off, shuddering at the memory of what he had seen.

Dugeen was examining the ripped and shattered pipeline. 'Look at it! Eighty gauge collodion, ripped like wet cardboard.'

Fenner caught Thawn's arm. 'We've got to evacuate,

Controller. Abandon the Refinery.'

Thawn thrust him away. 'Not while I'm Controller. Under no circumstances——'

'But just look at the damage, sir,' pleaded Dugeen. 'All done by just one tentacle—the equivalent of one of my fingers. Imagine what's going to happen if the creature decides to attack us in earnest!'

'Listen, Dugeen, I've put too much into this project to abandon it now. There's only one thing to do—find that creature and kill it!'

'And what about the broken pipeline?' asked Fenner.

'Switch to a secondary line and pump at half capacity until you've fixed it. Well, get on with it!'

Fenner and Dugeen went over to the controls, and a few minutes later the pumping machinery resumed its incessant throbbing.

Thawn stood at the window, staring out over the swamplands.

The Doctor, Romana and Rohm Dutt were being roped to a wooden framework, a kind of rack, laying in the middle of the temple floor. Behind them, Skart and Ranquin in full ceremonial regalia, were conducting a ceremony at the altar.

The Doctor watched them with interest. 'I don't remember that bit last night. Early Samoan influences, wouldn't you say? Interesting how traces of the old Earth cultures survive in their colonies, isn't it?'

'I'm more interested in my own survival at the moment,' muttered Romana. She had been lashed bodily to the wooden framework by lengths of creeper. Now her feet, stretched out in front of her were being tied to a kind of separate footboard that slid along the bottom. The footboard was lashed to more strands of glistening wet creeper, which was fastened at their other end to metal rings in the temple wall.

Next to her, the Doctor was being treated in the same way. So was Rohm Dutt, tied to the frame next to him.

The Doctor looked round the temple and in particular at a round glass window directly above them. 'This Temple's rather a hotch-potch of styles really. Still, I prefer it to perpendicular gothic.'

Rohm Dutt grunted as a burly warrior pulled his lashings tighter. 'Varlik, what is the seventh ritual?'

'It is the slowest death of all,' said Varlik sombrely.

Romana groaned. 'I knew it!'

'I tried to persuade the Chief that only the traitor Rohm Dutt deserved to be punished by the seventh ritual, that you others should suffer only the first.'

'What's that?' asked Romana faintly.

'It is very simple,' Varlik assured her. 'They just drop you into a pit and throw rocks on to you.'

'Oh, thanks,' said Romana weakly. 'It's nice to know who your friends are.'

'But Ranquin says your crimes are so great that Kroll will only be appeased by the length of your death agonies.'

'That window is quite out of place,' said the Doctor

suddenly. 'Not in character at all.'

'Will you please stop babbling about architecture,' said Romana crossly. 'We're having a serious conversation about our deaths.'

'Architecture's a serious subject too. Where did that window come from, Varlik?'

Varlik looked at him in puzzlement. 'It was brought from Delta Magna when this temple was built. It is very old ...'

'Well, I'd have sacked him,' said the Doctor.

Romana said, 'Sacked who?'

'The architect!'

'Are you trying to take my mind off things, Doctor? Because you're not succeeding!'

The Doctor grinned. 'Did I ever tell you about the time I met Dame Nelly Melba.'

'I don't want to hear about it.'

'She had this rather extraordinary party trick, you see.'

'I don't want to hear,' repeated Romana firmly.

By now Varlik's men had completed their work. All three captives were laying flat on their backs tied to the wooden frame. Their feet were lashed to the footboard, which in turn was tied by the wet swamp creepers to the iron rings set in the temple wall.

'Varlik, how long does this seventh ritual take?' asked Rohm Dutt fearfully.

Varlik looked down at him. 'That depends on the sun.'

'What's the sun got to do with it?'

Varlik pointed to the wet and glistening vines.

'These creepers grow in our swamp. They lengthen to absorb water, shrink to half their length or less when they are dry.'

The Doctor looked at the contraption to which they were tied. 'I see! The sun comes through the window and dries the creepers. Our bonds will tighten, and the length of creeper will shorten and pull the plank closer to the wall—and our feet with it, stretching us until we snap. How very ingenious. Well, at least I know the purpose of the window.'

'You'll be able to die happy then, won't you,' muttered Romana.

Varlik looked at the Doctor and Romana with a certain sympathy. 'I am sorry that this must happen. But if Kroll is not appeased by sacrifice, he will not help the People of the Lakes.'

'He didn't do much for you the last time he popped up,' pointed out the Doctor cheerfully. 'Killing the High Priest and swallowing the Symbol of Power.'

Ranquin and Skart came down from the altar. 'Is all prepared?'

Varlik bowed. 'All is prepared.'

Ranquin raised his hands and began to chant. 'O Great Kroll, defender and saviour. These despoilers and profaners of the temple are condemned to die by the Seventh Holy Ritual of the Old Book. Let their torments avert thy wrath from the People of the Lakes, thy true followers and believers. O Most Powerful One, so let it be!'

Ranquin leaned over the Doctor. 'Have you anything to say to the servants of Kroll before you die?'

'Why don't you just call the whole thing off? You've made your point.'

'Foolish levity,' said Ranquin sadly. 'Let us leave these sinners to their fate.'

'You're not leaving, surely. Aren't you going to stay and watch?'

'We are not savages. Your sufferings will be unpleasant to witness.'

'It'll be even more unpleasant to experience,' said the Doctor. 'Ranquin—what was the Symbol, the secret of Kroll's power?'

Ranquin hesitated. 'What do you know of such things, dryfoot?'

'Oh, I read about it somewhere,' said the Doctor vaguely.

'Kroll has the power of the Symbol,' Ranquin intoned. 'He knows all, sees all.'

'I know Kroll has it *now*. He must have, he swallowed it. But what *is* it?'

'The Symbol was a holy relic brought here by our ancestors at the time of the settlement.'

'What was its power?'

'He who holds the Symbol can see the future. The power revealed how the dryfoots would destroy Delta Magna with their machinery and their greed and the evils of their great cities. That is why our people came to settle here.'

'Your people were evicted from their homeland on Delta Magna, Ranquin. They had to come here— they had no choice.'

Ranquin looked curiously at him. 'Why do these

questions concern you, dryfoot—you who are about to die?'

'Oh, I just like to get things straightened out.'

Romana looked at the creepers. Already they had shrunk until the bodies of the three captives were stretched uncomfortably taut. 'Must you use expressions like that, Doctor. We're the ones being straightened out!'

Ranquin gave the Doctor a last puzzled stare and turned away. 'Your minds are bent, dryfoot. It is well that you die.' He went out of the Temple.

The Doctor sighed. 'He's got a bigoted mind and narrow little eyes. It's very hard to hypnotise people like that.'

Romana braced herself against the tug of the creepers. 'I see, so that's what you were trying to do?'

'I thought I might be able to get him to untie us—it's our only chance—well, almost our only chance.'

'How long will all this take?' grunted Rohm Dutt.

The Doctor shrugged. 'Hard to say. I don't know the contraction rate of that creeper.'

'I can feel it dragging on me already.'

'Bet you're sorry you didn't stay on Delta Magna now, eh?' said the Doctor unsympathetically. 'Who paid you to bring the natives useless guns? The truth now—it may be your last chance.'

Rohm Dutt paused, then said reluctantly. 'It was the Controller of the Refinery—Thawn. He wanted a good excuse to wipe them out.'

'And who do the Swampies *think* sent them the guns?'

'I told them the guns were sent by the Sons of Earth. I got a receipt from them too, marked with Ranquin's seal. Thawn wanted it to use to discredit the Swampies and the Sons of Earth afterwards.'

'Why?'

Rohm Dutt groaned as the creepers contracted further. 'Do you have to keep on asking so many questions at a time like this?'

'Why did Thawn want to discredit the Sons of Earth?'

'They're an organisation of cranks, back on Delta Magna. They support these primitives, want Thawn and his Refinery to pull out.'

'Why do they call themselves the Sons of Earth?' asked Romana.

The Doctor said, 'You know, that's a very good question, Romana. None of them can have seen Earth.'

'Mother Earth, they call it,' growled Rohm Dutt. 'They think colonising the planets was a mistake ... want us all to return to Earth ...' He groaned. 'My back—it's breaking ...'

'Imagination,' said the Doctor severely. 'That won't happen for quite some time yet.'

There was a distant roll of thunder. The Doctor's eyes lit up and he looked hopefully at the window. But the sunshine still streamed through, contracting the creeper—and the strain on the bodies of the captives grew greater and greater every moment.

The Doctor wondered how much longer they could last.

Thawn stood in the control room, looking at the sinister shape on the screen of the scanner. 'How far away is it now?'

'About six hundred yards,' said Dugeen grimly.

Thawn measured the image on the screen, did a few rapid calculations and looked up in astonishment. 'According to the scale of the scanner image that thing must be nearly half a mile wide!'

'Not far off. According to my calculations, the central mass is about a quarter of a mile in diameter by a hundred and forty feet high.'

Fenner came in and looked apprehensively at the screen. 'Anything happening?'

Thawn shook his head. 'It still hasn't moved.'

'I wonder what it looks like out of the water,' said Dugeen wonderingly.

Thawn remembered the sight of the monster rising from the swamps. 'What do you think it looks like? Very big, and very ugly. How's the repair work, Fenner?'

'The pump chamber's clear and the fans are working normally again.'

'Good. I want you to fix the main pipeline as soon as possible.' Thawn looked at the humped shape on the screen. 'Killing that thing's our first priority though.'

'How?' asked Fenner. 'How many depth charges did you find?'

'Thirty-five. Should be enough. Getting them to the creature is the main problem. We need to hit it with the whole lot at the same time.'

'That would mean going dangerously near,' objected Fenner.

'Exactly.'

There was a grim silence.

'It would help if we knew what it was,' said Dugeen. 'There's nothing that size back on Delta Magna—— Why don't we send a message back to Delta Magna, ask them for a rocket strike?'

Fenner shook his head. 'It would take too long. And anyway, we could send them its position now, but it could easily have moved by the time the missiles struck. It would have to be a low intensity strike, or we'd be caught in the blast area.'

'Those depth charges of yours,' said Fenner suddenly. 'Suppose we packed them all into one container, and sank it when it was directly over the creature?'

'How would we explode it?'

'We could use pressure detonators, that's easy enough.'

'Yes, but how would you sink the tank at exactly the right place?'

'We could fix a small charge to the bottom of the tank and fire it by remote control.'

'With a tank packed with depth charges and detonators,' jeered Thawn. 'The whole lot would go up at once—and us with it!'

'You were the one who wanted to use depth charges,' shouted Fenner, in sudden hysterical rage. 'I said all along it was too dangerous. We ought to evacuate now, before that thing comes back.'

'No,' said Thawn flatly.

There was another silence.

Dugeen glanced at the oscillating blips on the screen of his weather scanner. 'If anybody's interested, there's a hell of a big storm building up.'

'That's all we need,' said Fenner wearily. The storms on Delta Magna were ferocious, hours of driving winds, lashing rains and spectacular displays of thunder and lightning. 'Anyone want a drink?'

'No,' snapped Thawn. 'Batten down all exterior hatches and put the lightning conductors up.'

Dugeen's hands moved over the controls. 'Right away, sir. By the speed it's building up, this is going to be a big one.'

Thawn stared gloomily at the massive humped shape on the radar screen. Was it moving nearer? With a major rainstorm building up, it was impossible for them to make any kind of attack on it at least for the moment. They were caught between the monster and the storm.

All they could do was wait.

8

The Storm

Romana braced herself against the steady pull of the creepers, her body stretched like a bow-string. 'Doctor, it's getting hard to breathe.'

The Doctor was working steadily on the bonds that held his wrists. Unfortunately the concentration of the creepers was tightening them all the time. 'Don't give up, Romana.'

'My back,' moaned Rohm Dutt. 'It's breaking.'

The constant moans and complaints of the gun runner were almost the hardest part of their ordeal.

'Never mind,' said the Doctor cheerfully. 'Stretching's quite good for the spine—up to a point, that is.'

Romana suppressed a groan. 'I think I've passed that point already.'

The Doctor looked up at the window. The sky had darkened now. At least there was no more sunshine to hasten the drying of the creepers.

'Do you know I think we're in for a storm? Electrical storms on planetary satellites can be quite spectacular, you know.'

'What a pity we shan't be able to sit up and watch it,' said Romana sarcastically.

'Just try and relax your muscles, Romana.'

'It isn't my muscles, Doctor it's my spine. My vertebrae feel like beads on a piece of elastic.'

Nearby, in the Chief's hut, Varlik was arguing with his leader. 'It is not the fate of Rohm Dutt that troubles me. He is a traitor, he deserves to die. But the two others—they are not from the Refinery, and they have done us no real harm. Why must they be sacrificed?'

'They are dryfoots.' For Ranquin, it was answer enough.

'The Sons of Earth are dryfoots too,' Varlik pointed out. 'Yet we need their support for our cause on Delta Magna.'

'We need no one now,' said Ranquin arrogantly. 'We have Kroll!'

'Do we? I have listened to the words of the tall one. I begin to wonder.'

A lightning flash lit up the interior of the hut, and a massive thunderclap seemed to shake the entire stockade.

Ranquin went to the doorway and looked up at the darkening skies. Great drops of rain were beginning to fall ... Soon the torrential rain would begin lashing down. There was another lightning flash, another deafening thunderclap.

'Have a care, Varlik,' warned Ranquin. 'Kroll is our god and protector. He will punish those who doubt him.'

'Kroll killed Mensch—Mensch who was the loyalest

of his servants, Mensch who risked his life to spy on the dryfoots. Is that protection? If Kroll is our god, why has he attacked us in the past?'

'The ways of Kroll are mysterious, but we know this. He punishes those who disobey him—and he punishes those who displease his servants, of whom I am Chief! The strangers must die, Varlik. There is an end of the matter!'

Thawn stood in the observation dome of the Refinery, watching the approaching storm, hunching his massive body as though he could hold off the storm by sheer strength. The sky had darkened until it was more night than day. Great black cloud-formations were boiling in the sky and the lightning flashes and rolls of thunder were coming ever closer.

Thawn clenched his massive hands on the metal rail below the window. He would not fail. Despite the storm, the monster in the lagoon, the hostile Swampies and the interfering fools on Delta Magna, the Refinery would succeed. One day a dozen others would line the shores of the great lagoon, feeding the hungry millions, making him the most respected and honoured scientist on Delta Magna.

Thawn was an intense, lonely man and he had invested his whole career in the Refinery project. It could not, must not, fail.

He turned away from the window, hurried down the spiral staircase, along the corridor and into the control room.

Fenner and Dugeen were already at their post. During a storm, the Refinery was like a ship in a storm at sea. The violence of the storms was such that actual damage was a distinct possibility. Everyone stood by to take what counter-measures they could.

Fenner said, 'You were right, Dugeen. It's a big one.'

'You're telling me. The rain's blotting out everything on my scanners.'

Thawn checked through the standard precautions. 'Are the lightning conductor rods raised? We're going to need them.'

Fenner nodded. 'All checked.'

'Exterior hatches fastened? All doors secured?'

'Check.'

There was a brilliant lightning-flash, and a crash of thunder so loud that the entire room shook. 'Hold tight,' shouted Dugeen. 'Here we go!'

Rain lashed the Refinery, hurled against it by the driving winds.

They waited tensely as the thunderstorm raged all around them.

'I hope that creature's attack didn't cause any structural damage,' said Thawn grimly. 'If the wind gets inside here it could blow the place apart.'

The winds howled around them, and the rain drummed savagely on the roof.

Fenner shouted, 'Listen to that rain! I pity anyone out in that lot—even the Swampies!'

The Doctor looked up at the rain as it poured down on the roof, cascading away down the round glass window in streams. 'What we need are hailstones as big as bricks,' he muttered. 'Still, failing that ...'

The Doctor threw back his head and gave a high-pitched shriek.

Romana looked at him in scornful disbelief. 'Come on, Doctor, it isn't that bad yet!'

The Doctor ignored her. 'I'll just pitch it a little higher.' He shrieked again, a long, sustained, high-pitched note of such force and purity that it hurt the ears.

It did more than that. Suddenly the window shattered, showering the captives with broken glass. Rain poured into the Temple, drenching the three captives below.

'What happened, Doctor?' shouted Romana.

The Doctor beamed, rainwater running down his face. 'That was Dame Nellie Melba's party piece. Sonic vibration, you see. Mind you, she could only do it with wineglasses.'

'Don't see what good it's done getting us soaked,' grumbled Rohm Dutt.

'You will, old chap. You will!'

'The tension,' shouted Romana. 'It's easing already!'

The creepers were soaking up rainwater—and lengthening all the time.

'Come on both of you,' called the Doctor. 'Pull! We've got to stretch the creepers while they're still wet.'

They heaved back on the footboard, and with a final

yank the Doctor snatched his feet free of the loosening bonds. The creepers holding him to the frame were slackening too, and with a few desperate wriggles he struggled free, and got painfully to his feet. He looked down at Romana. 'There you are! Now you know what it feels like to be within an inch of death!'

'Stop congratulating yourself, Doctor, and get me up!'

'Patience, patience,' said the Doctor soothingly, and freed her from her bonds. 'Feet out, that's it ... there you are!'

He cut Rohm Dutt free as well. Seconds later they were all on their feet, stiff and aching, but alive.

'That's funny, Doctor,' said Romana.

'What is?'

'Well, all the time I was tied up, my nose was itching unbearably. Now it's stopped!'

'This is no time to be worrying about your nose.'

'Ah, but that's just it, you see, it's a very interesting example of displacement anxiety ...'

'Listen, if you want something to be anxious about, the storm seems to be easing. The Swampies will soon be coming out from under their umbrellas. I think it's time we got out of here!'

Dugeen looked up from his weather instruments. 'The storm's breaking up fast now. Just dropped four points on the scale.'

Fenner gave a sigh of relief. 'A few billion volts in that one!'

'It touched force twenty at the height. One of the worst I've seen. Anyone out on the lagoon wouldn't stand a chance.'

'Well there's not likely to be anyone on the lagoon is there? Not with our friend Jemima prowling about.'

Dugeen glanced at the radar screen and shouted. 'It is, too—on the prowl, I mean. Look!' The humped shape was moving rapidly across the screen. 'It's heading for the shore, moving fast!'

The storm had ended as suddenly as it began, and the returning sunshine sent up clouds of mist from the rain-soaked ground.

Ranquin strode across the dripping compound, followed by Skart and Varlik. Several huts had been badly damaged by the storm but no one had been killed. Kroll had protected his servants.

Ranquin led them into the Temple and stopped with a gasp of sheer disbelief. The wooden frame was empty, the sacrificial victims gone.

Varlik looked up at the shattered window. 'Kroll has been here. Kroll came in the storm, and took them.'

Skart shook his head. 'It is not possible. There would be more damage, traces of blood.'

Ranquin looked at the broken window, the loosened creepers trailing across the heavy wooden frame. 'They could not have freed themselves. Someone must have helped them.'

'Nobody here would help them,' protested Varlik.

89

Ranquin looked narrowly at him. 'Are you sure of that, Varlik? But a short time ago, *you* argued that two of the captives should be freed.'

'I asked you to spare the tall one and the girl from the Ritual,' said Varlik steadily. 'But that is all I did, Ranquin. I swear it.'

Ranquin glared suspiciously at him. 'By the powers I hold from Kroll, I shall learn the truth. But I tell you this—if the dryfoots are not found and sacrificed according to our Holy Ritual, then all our people will suffer the anger of Kroll.'

'They cannot have gone far,' said Varlik slowly. 'No dryfoot can find the secret paths through the swamps.'

'Go after them and find them,' ordered Ranquin. 'The dryfoots must die!'

9

Escape Through the Swamps

Cautiously the Doctor led them through the swamps, his eyes studying every inch of the ground in front of them. Romana glanced over her shoulder. Reeds were rustling behind them, a rustling not caused by wind. She caught a flash of sunlight on a spear-blade. 'Can't we go any faster, Doctor? I think they're coming after us.'

'We could, but I wouldn't advise it. One slip here, and you're in up to your ears.' The Doctor paused. 'The next bit of firm ground's just over there—I think! We'll have to jump!'

Romana looked dubiously at the spot the Doctor was indicating. 'Are you sure?'

'There's only one way to find out!' The Doctor took a flying leap and landed safely on firm ground. 'It's all right. Come on!'

Romana jumped, landing beside the Doctor.

Rohm Dutt hesitated.

'Come on, if you're coming,' shouted the Doctor. 'Or would you sooner wait for our friends?'

Clumsily, Rohm Dutt jumped, and landed beside them.

They hurried on their way.

Thawn and Fenner stood looking over Dugeen's shoulder at the radar scanner. At the moment it was completely blank.

Dugeen adjusted various controls with no success. 'Sorry, Controller, it's gone right off the scanner.'

'Well where is it then?'

'As far as I can tell, the thing just ploughed straight on into the swamp. It must be somewhere underneath it now.'

'Can't you get a track on it?'

'No sir. The swamp's got a viscosity level of around forty per cent solids. Under those conditions, the radar's blind.'

Fenner looked at the blank screen. 'The astonishing thing is it didn't seem to slow up at all when it left the lagoon. It seems to be able to move as easily through swamp-mud as through water.' He punched up a chart on a nearby readout screen. 'Now, it's moving on a bearing of ninety-seven degrees. You know where that's going to take it, Controller?'

'No—where?'

'Straight towards the Swampie Settlement!'

'Maybe it's just coincidence,' suggested Dugeen.

'Maybe it is. But it could have headed off in any direction. But it just happens to be heading straight for the Settlement—which means the Swampies have something of a problem.'

'But it couldn't possibly *know* the Settlement's there,' argued Dugeen. 'I mean, the place is miles away.'

'It knew Harg was in the pump chamber, didn't it? Maybe it's got a highly sensitive mechanism for detecting food.'

Thawn's heavy features broke into a smile. 'Maybe it has—in which case, as you say, the Swampies have rather a problem.'

Fenner looked curiously at him. 'You know I don't particularly like Swampies, Controller. But I can't say I really hate them either—not the way you do.'

'Oh, I don't hate them, Fenner. I just want them removed from the scene—permanently. I've spent years persuading the Government to back this project.' Thawn's voice rose to a hysterical shout. 'And now it's on the verge of success, I'm not going to be stopped by any lily-livered sentimentalising about the fate of a few primitive savages.' He drew a deep breath. 'I've got two problems at the moment—the Swampies, and that monster. If one of them wipes out the other, that's fine by me. I don't even care very much which one wins—because *I* shall exterminate the survivor!'

The green-skinned warriors ran lightly and confidently along the almost invisible paths through the swamp. They had no need to wait, and look, and feel their way. Like all their people, they had known the swamps from childhood, had learned almost to sense when ground was firm. Spears in hand, they followed the trail of the Doctor and his friends. Soon they would overtake them, and Kroll should have his sacrifice.

The air in the swamp was warm and humid, the reeds restricted vision to a few feet and the ground was soft and treacherous underfoot. It was like trying to escape blindfold through a tub of treacle, thought Romana. 'How much further, Doctor?'

'Not far. I hid the boat in some reeds by the main channel. As long as no one's moved it ...' Suddenly the Doctor held up his hand. 'Sssh!'

'What is it, Doctor?'

There was a strange, glutinous sucking sound. It seemed to come from just ahead of them.

'Listen,' said Romana. 'What's that noise?'

The sucking squelching sound became louder.

The Doctor pointed. 'Look!'

Just ahead of them, a whole section of path suddenly disappeared, sucked down beneath the marsh by some unseen force.

'We're being hunted,' whispered the Doctor.

'We know that,' growled Rohm Dutt. 'They've been on our trail for hours.'

'I don't mean by the Swampies—I mean by Kroll! He's here—*underneath the swamp*!' The Doctor looked round. 'Freeze, everybody. Don't so much as twitch an eyebrow.'

They all stood very still.

All around them the marsh seemed to heave and bubble. A line of subsidence moved across it, like the wake of some vast underwater shape. It seemed to be travelling towards them.

Rohm Dutt's nerve suddenly broke. He began

sprinting desperately across the swamp, leaping from tussock to tussock, blundering in and out of mud pools, crashing through the reeds like an elephant gone berserk.

An enormous grey tentacle rose out of the swamp, flicked around his waist, and plucked him out of existence. There was a dreadful bubbling scream, a squelching, sucking sound—then silence.

Romana covered her face with her hands. 'That was horrible, Doctor. Horrible!'

The Doctor put a consoling hand on her shoulder. 'Yes, it was. I told him not to move. Kroll hunts by surface vibrations, you see. He couldn't miss Rohm Dutt, not with him thumping about like that. Kroll's primarily a vegetarian—but just recently he seems to have learned that anything that actually moves is a potential source of wholesome nourishment.'

'Like us, you mean?'

'That's right. Or the Swampies. They'd better not get too close to their god——' The Doctor broke off. 'And speaking of Swampies, we'd better get a move on.'

There was a rustling in the reeds behind them—and it was getting nearer.

Varlik knelt by a patch of muddy ground. Two sets of tracks—the tall one and the girl. No sign of Rohm Dutt though—he must have split off from the others. It didn't matter. There were other hunting parties in the swamp. Varlik rose and beckoned his men onwards.

The Doctor and Romana picked their way through the swamp.

Despite the need for speed, they were careful to move as lightly as they could. With the death of Rohm Dutt fresh in their minds, they wanted to cause no heavy vibrations to summon Kroll from his lair beneath the swamp.

'We're here,' whispered the Doctor at last, and pointed. A path sloped away downwards through the reeds. At the end of it they could see the edge of the lagoon—and the Doctor's boat, still moored to its tree-root.

They ran swiftly down the bank and the Doctor held the boat steady while Romana jumped in. He scrambled in after her, cast off and paddled swiftly away.

A spear flashed across the lagoon, and thudded quivering in the side of the boat.

'Look, Doctor!' screamed Romana.

A band of Swampie warriors was pouring down the bank. Several of them threw spears, though luckily all missed. The Doctor paddled desperately, increasing the range as quickly as he could.

They saw Varlik leading the band. He pointed towards them and shouted an order. One of the warriors dived into the pool and swam strongly towards them, a knife between his teeth.

The Doctor paddled even harder, but soon the man was abreast of them. A green arm snaked out of the water, trying to overturn the boat.

The Doctor stopped paddling and discouraged their attacker with a fierce crack on the head with his paddle. The warrior fell back and the Doctor drove the boat onwards.

But the delay had lost them distance. Now another warrior was in the water.

The Doctor paddled desperately on. Then suddenly he stopped, and sat very still. Everything went quiet.

'What is it, Doctor?' whispered Romana.

'Look!'

Ahead of them the water began to boil and seethe and bubble. Something was rising out of the lagoon, something colossal, terrifying, malevolent.

Like a living mountain, Kroll rose from beneath the lagoon.

10

The Rocket

It was, thought the Doctor, quite the largest living creature he had ever seen. The immense blubbery grey sac of the body was supported on immensely long tentacles. There were no eyes—but somehow Kroll sensed the movement of the warrior swimming for the boat.

An incredibly long tentacle flicked out and plucked the man from the water, carried him screaming through the air and thrust him towards the monster's gaping mouth, where feeding mandibles seized him and thrust him inside.

'Freeze!' hissed the Doctor.

Romana froze.

They sat quite still, the boat drifting gently on the lagoon. The Swampie warriors on the bank threw themselves to the ground in terror—a fact which undoubtedly saved their lives.

With a monstrous bubbling and seething of the waters, Kroll sunk back beneath the lagoon.

Varlik and his warriors raised their heads, and seeing that Kroll had gone, they turned and fled.

In the boat, Romana let out a long, shuddering sigh. 'It's gone.'

The Doctor nodded. 'Yes, it's gone. For the moment ...'

'What a good thing you realised that it reacts to movement!'

'Yes, wasn't it?' The Doctor raised his paddle. 'Still, let's get out of here, before it gets hungry again.'

With slow careful strokes, the Doctor drove the boat across the lagoon.

Thawn was pacing up and down the control room. 'We've got to find out what that creature's *doing*. Dugeen, train a scanner receptor aerial on the Settlement. If that thing does attack the Swampies we may be able to see something from here.'

'Right, sir.'

'The Settlement's over two miles away,' protested Fenner.

'Even so, if it's as big as we think it is ...' Thawn went over to a separate control console.

Dugeen looked up puzzled. 'What are you doing, sir?'

'Just checking the next orbit shot is charged and ready to fire.'

'Everything's ready, sir. I checked it myself. But the next orbit shot isn't due for two hours, Controller.'

'This time it might be a little early——'

Dugeen interrupted him. 'Look, sir. I'm getting something on the screen.'

There was a bubbling, sucking sound, a high whistling scream and the immense grey shape of Kroll rose from the swamp beside the Settlement.

In the stockade below, Swampies fled in terror in all directions. Kroll's mighty tentacles flicked out, snatching them up and thrusting them into the gaping mouth. Once again Kroll was manifesting himself to his worshippers.

The horrific scene at the Settlement was visible though blurred and miniaturised, on the screen of the Refinery scanners.

Fenner gave a whistle of sheer disbelief. 'It is as big as we thought—bigger!'

Thawn was busy at the rocket control console. 'A hundred tons of compressed protein will still smash it to fragments.'

Fenner came over to join him. 'What are you planning to do?'

'I'm going to blast our next rocket shot right into the middle of that overgrown octopus.'

Dugeen was horrified. 'You can't do that, sir!'

'Oh can't I?' Thawn adjusted the controls. 'Maximum depression bearing nine seven ...'

'You're mad,' whispered Dugeen. 'An orbital rocket at two miles range? Think what it'll do to the Settlement!'

Thawn chuckled. 'Ever heard that old expression—killing two birds with one stone?'

Fenner came to Dugeen's support. 'Controller, think what you're doing.'

'I have thought.'

'You know how thin the atmosphere is here. The rocket fuel will go up. The explosion could cause a fireball big enough to asphixiate us.'

'I doubt it.' Thawn went on working.

'You doubt it? Are you sure? Have you worked out the risk?'

Thawn threw a switch. 'Countdown commencing. Places, everybody.'

Dugeen turned to Fenner. 'He's mad I tell you. We've got to stop him!'

Fenner shrugged and turned away. 'He's the Controller. It's his responsibility, not mine.'

Dugeen renewed his appeal. 'Controller, please, you can't do this. You'll be killing innocent people.'

'They're only Swampies.'

'Call them what you like. They're people, no different from you or me.'

'They're very different, I assure you Dugeen.' Thawn's voice hardened. 'Now, get back to your place.'

'No.'

'You refuse to obey my lawful orders?'

Dugeen stood his ground. 'On moral grounds, sir. Look, if you fire that rocket it isn't just the monster that will die. You'll be destroying a civilisation that's older than our own.'

'The Swampies? Civilised? You know, Dugeen, you're talking like one of those fanatics from the Sons of Earth.'

'We are not fanatics,' shouted Dugeen in sudden

rage. 'All life began on Mother Earth—and all life is sacred!' He tried to pull Thawn away from the controls.

Thawn shoved him back, and produced a blaster from under his tunic. 'I'm giving you one last chance, Dugeen.'

Undeterred by the gun, Dugeen went on struggling.

Thawn smashed him to the ground with a savage blow from the butt.

He turned on Fenner. 'Now, are *you* going to give me an argument?'

'No, Controller,' said Fenner woodenly. He went to his place. 'Countdown commences in two minutes.'

Thawn sank back into his own control chair. 'Right. Keep a track on that thing for me.'

The Doctor and Romana came into the pump room, looked at the gaping hole in the shattered pipe.

'Kroll?' whispered Romana.

The Doctor nodded. 'Looks like it. Let's see if there are any survivors.'

As they moved along the corridor to the control room they heard angry voices.

The Doctor paused outside the door and was just in time to hear the argument between Thawn and Dugeen, and to see the younger man struck down. He turned and hurried away.

Romana followed him. 'Where are you going, Doctor?'

'The rocket silo. If he fires that orbital shot there'll be nothing left of Kroll, or the Swampies either. If I try and stop him from the control room he'll just shoot me down. Got to do it from out here somehow.'

The Doctor ran round to the rear of the Refinery. When he reached the rocket silo, he set to work, turning the wheel that opened the metal door of the concrete firing bay. 'Thawn's using the over-ride firing mechanism. There must be some way of disconnecting it from this end.'

'Doctor, if the rocket is fired while you're in there——'

'Yes,' said the Doctor thoughtfully. 'Maybe we'd better say goodbye now! Goodbye, Romana.'

He slipped into the firing bay.

'Doctor!' called Romana. She ran in after him.

The firing bay was little more than a concrete walled pit, holding the orbital rocket on its steel gantry. Normally the rocket would have been aimed directly upwards but now it was tilted over at an angle, aimed like some great space cannon at the Settlement.

The Doctor climbed quickly up a narrow steel ladder, and opened a hatch in the rocket's side, just below the firing vents.

Studying the control panel for a moment, he set to work.

'Sixty seconds to countdown,' said Fenner.

Thawn nodded. 'Fire primaries.'

'Primary ignition functioning.'

'Continue countdown.'

'Fifty seconds.'

Intent on their tasks, neither Thawn nor Fenner noticed the huddled figure of Dugeen beginning to stir.

There was a growing rumble as the rocket burners began to heat up. Clouds of white vapour enveloped the Doctor, as he perched precariously on his ladder, working on the control panel with his sonic screwdriver.

Romana stood looking up from the ground below. 'Doctor, we're too late, they've commenced ignition. Come down!'

'Get out of here, Romana. Just get out!'

Feverishly the Doctor went on working.

The rocket hull was hot to the touch now and there was a fiery glow from the vents. The Doctor's head was swimming with the heat, and he almost fell from the ladder ...

'Thirty seconds to countdown,' said Fenner. 'Burner eight hundred and increasing.'

Suddenly Dugeen was on his feet, lurching towards the main control console. 'No, Thawn, I won't let you do it.'

Thawn raised his blaster. 'Dugeen, if you touch that abort button, I swear I'll kill you.'

'Then kill me. But you're not going to wipe out an entire race as well.'

As Dugeen hurled himself forward and pressed the abort button, Thawn fired.

11

Countdown

The force of the laser blast hurled Dugeen across the room, and slammed him against the wall. He stared at Thawn with astonished disbelief for a moment, then slid slowly to the ground ...

Thawn glared wildly at Fenner. 'I warned him. You heard me warm him!'

Fenner went over to the body, knelt to examine it, straightened up. 'That was murder! Cold-blooded murder.'

Thawn wasn't listening to him. He was staring at the control console, where the digital clock was still flicking away the last seconds of the countdown. *Twelve ... eleven ... ten ...* 'Look! The countdown hasn't stopped. *It hasn't aborted.*'

Fenner looked at the instrument panel. 'The master cut-out's failed. You killed him for nothing.'

The counter clicked on. *Five ... four ... three ... two ...*

The Doctor had removed the front of the control panel only to reveal an immensely complicated mass of solid state circuitry. There wasn't a hope of reconnecting it in the seconds now available. 'When in doubt—cut everything,' thought the Doctor, and smashed his sonic screwdriver against the circuit panel. It exploded in a shower of sparks, hurling the Doctor from the ladder to the concrete floor below.

Two ... one ... the countdown clock froze.

Thawn stared at it in amazement. 'I don't understand. First it didn't abort then——'

Fenner was studying the read-out screen. 'According to the computer, there's a fault in the primary ignition panel—on the rocket itself.'

Thawn turned to the door. 'We can soon fix that!'

'Too late.' Fenner nodded towards the radar screen, where the massive, humped shape was subsiding towards the bottom of the frame. 'It's submerging again, back into the swamp. You're not going to hit it with your rocket down there.'

Thawn shot an angry glance at Dugeen's huddled body. 'If that spineless fool hadn't interfered ...'

'He'd still be alive, wouldn't he?' There was cold anger in Fenner's usually calm voice. 'That was murder, Controller.'

'It was justifiable homicide. You heard me warn him not to touch that abort button. He was trying to commit an act of sabotage.'

'He didn't like your methods. That does not make him a saboteur. I'm reporting what happened the moment we get back.'

'He was a spy,' blustered Thawn. 'A spy from the Sons of Earth. It's obvious now—they sent him here to cripple my project, any way they could.'

'Is that a reason for killing him?'

Thawn hammered a fist on to the console. 'All right, Fenner, that will do! No doubt you can make things sound bad for me when we get back to Delta Magna. But suppose we don't get back, eh? Suppose that thing destroys us both? That'll be *his* fault—not mine!' With a final glare at Dugeen's body, he marched for the door.

'Where are you going?'

'To check over that rocket—just in case we get another chance!'

The Settlement was wrecked, the stockade and most of of the flimsy grass huts smashed to fragments, by Kroll's flailing tentacles. Many of the People of the Lakes were dead, snatched into the gaping maw of Kroll, to feed his unending hunger.

A few survivors huddled together in the ruins, grouped around their Chief.

Ranquin was fighting for his survival, and for his beliefs.

'Why?' demanded Varlik. 'Why did this happen, Ranquin. Why has Kroll turned against us?'

The Chief's voice was assured and steady, and the light of fanaticism still burned in his eyes. 'It is our punishment for letting the dryfoots escape us.'

'But when we almost had them, it was Kroll himself who came between us.'

'It was a test. The great one was testing your faith.'

'A test?' shouted Varlik furiously. 'Nual was killed there—and how many others have died here today?'

Ranquin's faith was unshaken. 'Kroll took their lives, in place of the sacrifice *we* failed to give him. But he will not be appeased until that sacrifice is made. The dryfoots must be found—and sacrificed. Only then will Kroll restore his favour to his people. *Where are they?*'

'Our scouts report they were heading for the Refinery.'

Ranquin folded his arms, his face implacable. 'Then we must follow. The dryfoots must die!'

The Doctor lay flat on his back on the concrete floor of the rocket bay. Romana knelt beside him, trying to revive him. 'Doctor, wake up! Are you all right?'

The Doctor sat up so suddenly he made her jump. 'What? Yes, of course I am. Just a touch of oxygen starvation. Blacked out for a few seconds.'

'A few minutes, more like it.'

'Well I needed the rest—minutes! Did you say minutes?'

'Minutes,' said Romana firmly.

The Doctor jumped to his feet. 'We'd better get out of here!' He looked up at the rocket, with its shattered control panel. 'If we're found loitering, somebody might put two and two together.'

He opened the door and found himself facing Thawn's blaster. The Doctor backed away. 'You're putting two and two together, aren't you?'

Thawn smiled with grim satisfaction. 'So you came back.'

'I remembered I went off without saying goodbye properly. This is my friend Romana, by the way. You remember, I was looking for her?'

'Hello,' said Romana politely.

Thawn ignored her. 'And what are you doing here this time?'

'Just closing the blast door. It really shouldn't have been left open like that,' said the Doctor severely. 'Very dangerous.'

'And who opened it, I wonder?'

'The cleaning lady?'

'I've no time for games,' said Thawn abruptly. 'Put your hands up where I can see them, and walk straight ahead of me—both of you.'

'Haven't you forgotten something?'

'What?'

'You didn't say "Don't make any sudden moves".'

'Don't make any sudden moves,' repeated Thawn humourlessly.

Stepping aside, he waved them towards the door with the blaster. 'Now get moving—straight to the control room.'

The Doctor and Romana raised their hands and obeyed.

The pump-room window was thrust open by a green hand. Varlik slid silently over the sill, and dropped into the room. He looked round for a moment, and then gave a low whistle.

Ranquin followed him through the window, then a handful of warriors—all that Ranquin had been able to persuade to accompany them. The others were hiding in the swamps, terrified Kroll would reappear.

There was a whirr and a thud as the pumping machinery began a new cycle.

Ranquin jumped. 'What is that?'

'Machinery,' said Varlik. 'It is only machinery.'

Ranquin glared angrily around the room. 'This place is an abomination.'

Varlik knew more about technology and had less fear of it. 'On Delta Magna all the dryfoots live in these metal boxes.'

'When we have completed our task, I shall ask Kroll to destroy this place,' said Ranquin grandly.

'And why should Kroll do as you ask?'

Ranquin glared angrily at his rebellious war chief. 'What is this insolence, Varlik?'

'If Kroll is the Great One, and you are but his servant . . .'

'While the People of the Lakes serve and do honour to Kroll, he will protect us against those who invade our waters.'

'Kroll has destroyed our village, killed most of our people. Was that to protect us?'

'These are blasphemous questions, Varlik!'

'I speak only what is in all our minds, Ranquin.'

There was a murmur of agreement from the others.

Desperately Ranquin fought to regain control ... 'Now hear me, all of you! We promised Kroll the lives of the two dryfoots who profaned his Temple. We failed to keep that promise!'

Ranquin paused impressively. 'I tell you this. Kroll will not rest easily beneath the waters, he will not cease to punish us until we have sacrificed the dryfoots, and he has eaten of their souls. Now, follow me!'

Raising his spear, Ranquin strode away.

For a moment Varlik hesitated, and so did the others. But their world had been shattered and Ranquin's belief was all they had to cling to now. Silently, they followed him down the corridor.

The Doctor and Romana reached the control room just as Fenner was dragging Dugeen's body into an adjoining storeroom.

The Doctor looked down at the body. 'I don't think that was necessary.'

'Neither do I,' said Fenner. He dragged the body into the store room, came out and closed the door.

'He tried to interfere, Doctor,' said Thawn. 'Just as you have interfered.' He glared wildly at them.

'You've no proof of that.'

'You were in the silo. The blast door to the firing bay was open, and there was a malfunction in the orbit shot.'

'Circumstantial evidence?' said Romana feebly.

'Well it satisfies me.' The hand that held the blaster was shaking with rage. 'You're saboteurs, both of you. There's no reason why I shouldn't execute you both now!'

'I wouldn't,' said Fenner laconically.

'And why not?'

'Because we're going to need all the help we can get. Take a look at that!'

He pointed to the radar screen. The massive shape of Kroll had risen again from the depths.

'Oh, look,' said the Doctor softly. 'It's coming this way!'

'That's right,' snapped Fenner. 'And this time it's coming to attack *us*!'

The Doctor nodded his agreement. 'You're probably right—I doubt if it's coming to shake hands, anyway.'

Fenner said, 'We'd better send an SOS to Delta Magna right away. They'll send a shuttle craft to get us out of here.'

The new crisis was almost too much for Thawn's already-slipping control. 'Shut up, all of you!' he screamed. 'How do you know it's coming to attack us? It it was going to do that, it would have come here *before* it attacked the Settlement.'

'Maybe it's saving you for pudding?' suggested the Doctor.

This flippancy in face of the threat to his Refinery was too much for Thawn. He swung round on the

Doctor, aiming the blaster at his head. 'I warned you, Doctor.' His voice was trembling with hysterical fury. 'I told you to shut up. Now I'm going to shut you up —for ever!'

Thawn's finger tightened on the trigger.

12

The Power of Kroll

As he looked at the gaping muzzle of the blaster and at the mad eyes above it, the Doctor realised that at last he'd made one joke too many.

A spear flashed across the room, and thudded into Thawn's heart.

Thawn stared at the jutting spear in astonishment, then fell dead to the floor, the blaster clattering from his hand.

The Doctor turned to see Ranquin in the doorway, Varlik and his warriors behind him.

The Doctor raised his hands pacifically. 'All right, all right, we surrender.' He nodded amiably at Ranquin. 'What do we get this time? The Eighth Holy Ritual?'

In all the excitement nobody noticed that the humped image on the scanner was now so large that it blotted out the entire screen ...

Kroll rose from the lagoon in all his terrifying majesty, and loomed over the frail metal structure that rose from the water's edge. He could not see it, because

Kroll was blind, but he could *sense* it, feel the strange alien vibration of the machinery. The vibration meant movement, movement meant life—and to Kroll life was no more than food, fuel for his ravenous bulk.

Swaying on his tentacles Kroll lurched towards the Refinery ...

Ranquin was making a long rambling speech, accusing the Doctor of blasphemy and profanation, and of bringing down the wrath of Kroll on the People of the Lakes—presumably by not letting himself be meekly sacrificed.

'Many have died because of you, dryfoot,' Ranquin concluded bitterly. 'You have been promised to Kroll —and now he shall have you. Kroll, who is all wise, all seeing ...'

'All baloney!' interrupted the Doctor rudely. 'Kroll couldn't tell the difference between you and me and half an acre of dandelion and burdock—it's all food, and that's all that interests him.'

'I tell you Kroll will not be denied!' screamed Ranquin. He snatched a spear from one of his warriors, raised it—and fell reeling as a massive weight crashed against the Refinery.

Kroll had arrived.

The imense grey sac that was Kroll's body pressed against the Refinery tower, his tentacles wrapped angrily around it. The metal felt hard and alien to his touch, yet somehow he sensed there was life, food, somewhere inside it.

With a whistling roar of rage and frustration, Kroll's tentacles explored the structure, seeking for his prey.

The entire Refinery was swaying and shaking with the fury of Kroll's attack and Ranquin and his warriors huddled together in terror.

'What are we going to do?' shouted Fenner. 'Just sit here while that thing smashes the place to pieces?'

'Ask Ranquin,' suggested the Doctor calmly. 'He's supposed to be the Kroll expert.'

'You have brought death to us all, dryfoot,' screamed Ranquin.

'Oh, so that's your expert opinion is it?' grumbled the Doctor. 'It's all my fault! You know, Romana, I think if we—Romana?'

Romana was standing just outside the door, looking through the corridor window. 'Romana, come back in here,' called the Doctor.

Romana peered out. She was trying to get a good look at Kroll. It was difficult actually to see much since the monster's bulk obscured most of the window. 'I just want to *see* it, Doctor.'

He ran into the corridor after her. *'Come away from that window!'*

'It's all right, Doctor, it doesn't know we're here——' The window shattered in a shower of plasti-glass, and an enormous grey tentacle came grop-ing through.

The Doctor grabbed Romana's arm, yanked her back into the control room, and closed the door behind them. 'If it doesn't know we're here, it's making some pretty shrewd guesses!'

The door shuddered as the tentacle thumped against it. 'That door's not going to hold,' shouted Fenner. 'It's got us trapped.'

'Now, now, Fenner, don't give up,' said the Doctor cheerfully. 'Can you get the centrifuge running?'

'Yes, I suppose so. Why?'

'*Switch it on!*'

'Why? The feeder-tanks only half full. All it'll do is kick up a racket!'

'Exactly Fenner—noise! Kroll hunts by sensing vibration. Let's give him some to think about. Confuse him with noise and he won't detect us so easily!'

Fenner switched on the centrifuge. Soon the roaring whine of its machinery joined the steady throbbing of the pumping system.

The heaving grey mass of Kroll's body shuddered wildly as the Refinery began to vibrate. Maddened by the sound, the monster lashed at the steel platform in fury, trying to find and destroy the source of the vibration.

The tentacle outside the control room whipped back through the window, and joined the others in their flailing attack ...

Romana listened at the door. 'I think it's gone, Doctor.'

'Yes, but for how long? When it gets tired of attacking metal girders, it'll come looking for food again.'

Ranquin straightened up, trying to retrieve his lost dignity. 'The Great One is merciful. Kroll has heard my prayer.'

'All Kroll has heard is the sound of dryfoot machinery,' said Varlik scornfully.

The Doctor leaned over Fenner. 'Can you make any more noise?'

'I could start the compressors. they make enough row. And the emergency Klaxons ...'

'That's the idea. Give it everything you've got, Fenner. All the noise you can make. Just keep it busy!'

Fenner's hands moved over the controls and soon the steady thump, thump, thump, of the compressors joined the throbbing of the pumps and the high-pitched whine of the centrifuge. The wail of the sirens added to the din.

Ignoring the row, the Doctor went over to the door and slid it cautiously open. The corridor was clear. He took the Tracer out of his pocket and stood for a moment, bracing himself.

Romana went over to him. 'Where are you going, Doctor?'

The Doctor grinned ruefully. 'To test a theory. All theories have to be tested sometime. You stay here—just in case I'm wrong!'

'Wrong about what?'

'About Kroll—and the symbol of his power.'

The Doctor disappeared down the corridor.

When the Doctor had gone, Ranquin shouted, 'Come, my people. Let us leave this place of abomination to be destroyed by Kroll. The Great One will not harm his true servants.'

He led his warriors away from the control room and through the shuddering, vibrating steel corridors until they reached the pump room where they had first entered.

As they crossed the threshold, a flailing tentacle thrust through the shattered hole in the main pipeline.

Varlik and the others leaped back, but Ranquin moved forward, his face ecstatic. 'Master, hear the voice of thy servant Ranquin. Great Kroll, defender and saviour of thy People of the Lakes, let not thy wrath fall upon thy true servant.'

As if responding to Ranquin's voice, the tentacle groped hungrily for him.

Ranquin fell to his knees, holding up his hands in supplication. 'Great One, we ask only that the dry-foots and all their abominations be crushed by thy mighty power. Take *them* as thy sacrifice and spare thy true servant.' The tentacle coiled around Ranquin's body and dragged him screaming into the pipeline.

Varlik and the others turned and fled in terror.

The worship of Kroll was ended.

The Doctor ran along the corridors until he found a steel ladder leading to the upper level. He climbed it, opened a metal door and found himself on the catwalk that ran round the Refinery superstructure.

He was within a few feet of the body of Kroll. Pulling sluggishly, the colossal sphere of the monster's underbelly blotted out the horizon.

Tracer outstretched, the Doctor advanced on the monster, like a knight attempting to attack the most colossal of dragons. He switched on the Tracer and its electronic hum shot up to maximum.

The Doctor drew a deep breath. 'Well, I've had a happy life. Can't really complain. Nearly seven hundred and sixty, not a bad age . . .'

A stray tentacle lashed blindly over the railing, sweeping him off his feet—and knocking the Tracer from his hand. It rolled across the metal floor.

The Doctor leaped for it, but the tentacle wound round his body dragging him towards the edge of the platform—towards the waiting maw of Kroll, whose feeding-mandibles waved hungrily.

As he was dragged past the Tracer, the Doctor made a last frantic lunge and managed—just—to curl his fingers round the slender wand.

The tentacle dragged him to the edge of the platform and the Doctor lunged like a swordsman, thrusting the Tracer deep into the rubbery grey underbelly of the monster.

The result was extraordinary.

For a moment the great globular body, the flailing

tentacles, the gaping mouth of Kroll were irradiated with fierce blue fire.

Kroll vanished.

The Doctor stood alone on the platform, the Tracer in his hand. Attached to the end of the Tracer was a large, irregularly-shaped crystal—the fifth segment of the Key to Time.

The Doctor heaved a great sigh of relief. Detaching the segment, he went back inside the Refinery.

In the control room, Romana and Fenner, were waiting for him. Varlik and the other warriors were there too. They had fled back there from the pump room after Ranquin's death.

Fenner switched off the machinery, and a kind of astonished silence filled the control room.

The Doctor held up the crystal and beamed at Romana. 'There you are—the fifth segment.' He slipped it into his pocket.

Romana was overjoyed. 'Well done, Doctor!'

Varlik was staring in astonishment at the Tracer. 'You killed Kroll ... *with that stick?*'

The Doctor slipped the Tracer into his pocket. 'It's rather a special sort of stick.'

Fenner wasn't sharing in the general rejoicing. Instead he was hunched worriedly over his instrument console. 'Doctor, come here!'

The Doctor ambled across. 'What is it, old chap?'

'Something's blocking the firing bay. The whole

section seems to be—buckled.'

'Well, Kroll's been smashing the place about a bit. Bound to be some damage. Don't worry about it, Fenner. You don't need a firing bay any more. No more Kroll, no more protein source, no more orbit shots ... no more Refinery, come to that. It's all over.'

In a dull voice Fenner said, 'The computer doesn't know that, Doctor.'

Romana came over to join them. 'You mean it'll go on running things by itself?'

'That's how it was designed. The next shot is due in about fifty seconds. And it's already started the count-down.'

The Doctor rubbed his chin. 'I see. And if it tries to launch a rocket with the firing bay blocked ...'

'The whole place will blow up,' Fenner said fatalistically.

'Stop the computer,' suggested Romana.

'I've already tried. The manual over-ride and abort systems aren't functioning any more.'

The Doctor said guiltily, 'I know. I disconnected them in the firing bay.'

'Can't you reconnect them?' asked Romana.

'What? In fifty seconds.'

'Forty seconds,' said Fenner grimly.

'Forty seconds? Right, there's only one thing to do!'

The Doctor ripped the top of the inspection hatch and studied the maze of wires and circuitry within.

'I'll have to reverse the polarity and fuse the entire mechanism.'

He ripped out first one power cable then another and studied them thoughtfully. 'Let's hope these are the right ones.'

He touched the bared ends together. There was a bang and a flash and most of the console exploded in a shower of sparks.

Fenner looked at the countdown clock. The figures registered 02.01—and then stopped.

The Doctor's eyes were closed and he was standing perfectly still as if turned to stone.

'Doctor?' said Romana worriedly. 'Are you all right?'

The Doctor gave himself a tremendous shake, like a dog coming out of the water. He opened his eyes. 'Yes, I think so.'

'You might have been killed.'

'Yes,' said the Doctor thoughtfully. 'I suppose I might! Time to say goodbye, I think Romana. Let's go.'

Fenner looked round the control room and shook his head dazedly. 'Well, it looks like the end of this place.'

'It is finished, then?' asked Varlik.

'That's right,' said Fenner sardonically. 'You can have Delta Three back now—and as far as I'm concerned you're welcome to it.'

'Those of us who still live,' said Varlik sombrely. 'But we shall survive.' He led his warriors away.

The Doctor sidled towards the door.

'Where are you going?' asked Fenner.

'We must be on our way, too,' said the Doctor vaguely.

'That's right,' said Romana briskly. 'We've got a lot to do, haven't we, Doctor?'

'We have indeed.' The Doctor paused, taking a last look round the control room, and at the bemused Fenner. 'You'd better send a message to Delta Magna. They'll send someone to pick you up—eventually!'

'And what do I do till then?'

'You'll just have to lead a simple natural life for a while. Try it—you might even like it. Have you got food stores and medical supplies here?'

'Well, yes, but——'

'You could give Varlik and the other survivors some help. I think they'll need it. You could even teach them that there are better things to do with their lives than worship Kroll.'

Fenner opened his mouth to make an outraged protest—but the Doctor and Romana had gone.

Grumbling to himself, Fenner composed an urgent SOS message and sent it by sub-space radio to Delta Magna. He dragged Thawn's body into the store-room and laid it beside Dugeen. He thought about the Doctor's suggestion. 'Me! Some kind of Swampie missionary!' he grumbled. Then he began checking through the supplies of food and medicine. It would be something to do, till they came and took him home.

Epilogue

The Doctor moored his boat to a projecting tree root, helped Romana out and stood looking around him.

'This way, I think.'

'No, Doctor,' Romana pointed. 'That way!'

'Nonsense! I happen to have an unerring sense of direction, Romana. You should know that by now.'

The Doctor stepped determinedly forward and sank into swamp mud up to his knees. Romana helped him to pull free.

'Er, this way, I think,' said the Doctor and set off in the direction she'd indicated. Romana smiled to herself and followed him.

They picked their way through the swamp, heading for the knoll where they had left the TARDIS.

As they walked along, Romana asked, 'Doctor, how did you know the fifth segment was a part of Kroll?'

'Oh, well, it all seemed to add up,' said the Doctor vaguely. 'For a start there was the Tracer reading— wherever the segment was, we were right on top of it. And we know who was lurking under the swamp when we arrived, don't we?'

'Kroll?'

'Kroll! Then there was the sacred book, the one we found in the Temple. You remember it talked about the symbol of Kroll's power? It seemed pretty obvious that was the segment.'

'And the book said Kroll swallowed it!'

'That's right. Along with the High Priest, presumably. Of course, Kroll wasn't nearly so big then—just your ordinary giant squid. It was the segment that caused him to mutate, just go on growing and growing. Trouble is, he got so big the lake couldn't feed him any more. He had to surface and start hunting for food ... Hello, look at this!'

The Doctor stooped down and scooped something out of the water. He held it out to Romana. It was a tiny squid-like creature, wriggling furiously in his hand.

'A baby Kroll,' said the Doctor delightedly. 'There must be hundreds of these little creatures wriggling about by now. Cellular regeneration you see. Taking away the segment transformed one big Kroll into lots of little ones.'

'They won't all grow up like Kroll will they?' asked Romana in alarm.

'No, no, no, nothing like Kroll. These will be ordinary giant squids. Nothing to worry about—unless you're a High Priest of course!' He tossed the squid into a pool with a plop. 'No, there'll never be another Kroll. It was the segment that did it all ...'

Romana pointed to a flash of blue amidst the reeds. 'Look Doctor, the TARDIS!'

The Doctor led the way to the police box and opened the door. Immediately a delighted electronic barking broke out. 'Down K9, down!' shouted the Doctor. 'It's all right, we're back—*and* we've found the segment.'

Romana followed him into the TARDIS, and the door closed behind them.

A few minutes later, there was a wheezing groaning sound and the police box faded away.

One adventure was over, another about to begin.

The search for the sixth and last segment of the Key to Time.

It was to be the most astonishing quest of all ...